Monsters, Mayhem
and a Sprinkling of
Crumbs!

For Anna & Charlotte xx – TC
For Pete & Celia, with love – AP

STRIPES PUBLISHING LIMITED
An imprint of Little Tiger Group
1 Coda Studios, 189 Munster Road,
London SW6 6AW

Imported into the EEA by Penguin Random House Ireland,
Morrison Chambers, 32 Nassau Street, Dublin D02 YH68

A paperback original
First published in Great Britain in 2013

Text copyright © Tracey Corderoy, 2013
Illustrations copyright © Ali Pye, 2013

ISBN: 978-1-84715-380-7

A CIP catalogue record for this book is available from the British Library.

Printed and bound in the UK.

MIX
Paper from
responsible sources
FSC® C020471

The Forest Stewardship Council® (FSC®) is a global, not-for-profit organization
dedicated to the promotion of responsible forest management worldwide. FSC®
defines standards based on agreed principles for responsible forest stewardship
that are supported by environmental, social, and economic stakeholders.
To learn more, visit www.fsc.org

2468109753

Monsters, Mayhem and a Sprinkling of Crumbs!

Tracey Corderoy

Illustrated by Ali Pye

LITTLE TIGER

LONDON

Inventions 390–394

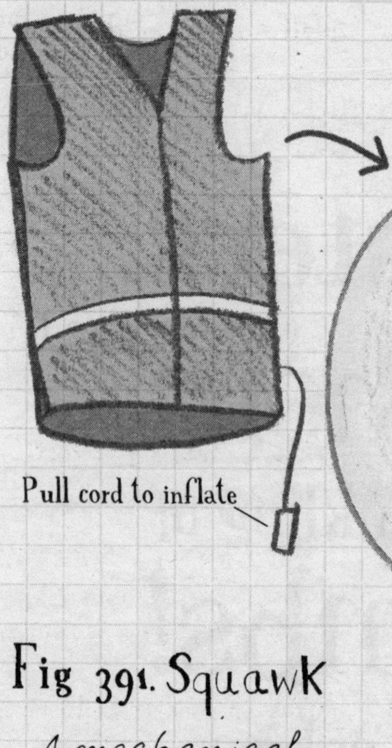

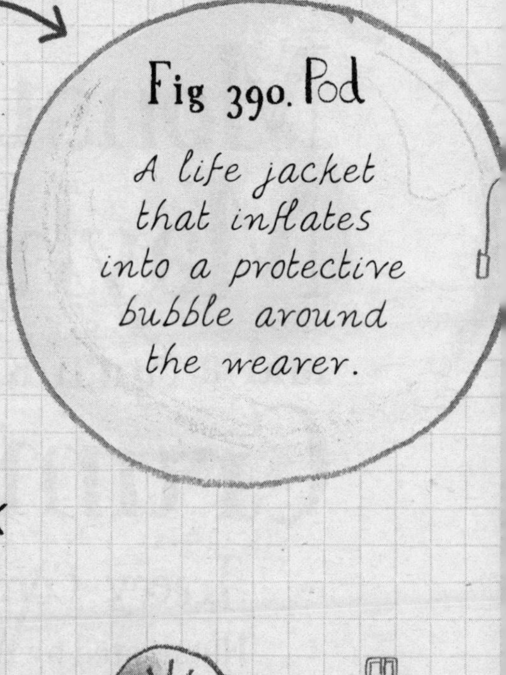

Fig 390. Pod

A life jacket that inflates into a protective bubble around the wearer.

Pull cord to inflate

Fig 391. Squawk

A mechanical spy-bird that shoots aerial video and beams the footage to Otto's tracker watch.

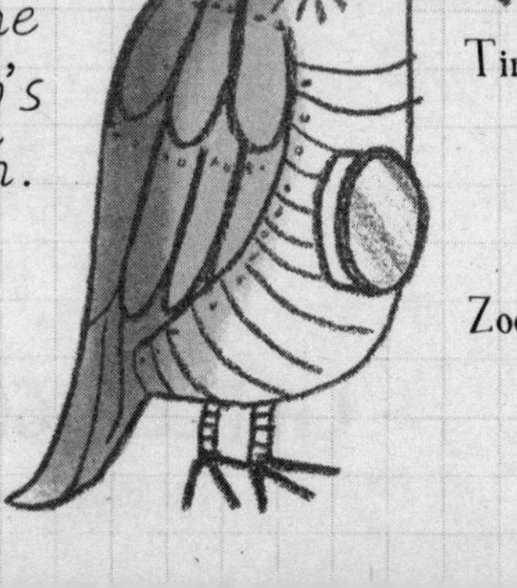

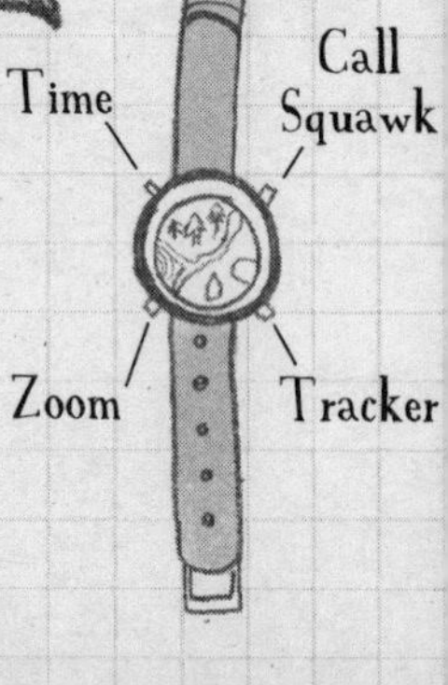

Time

Call Squawk

Zoom

Tracker

Fig 392.
Creeper-Sneakers

Gravity-defying shoes for walking on walls and hanging upside down.

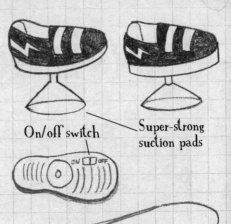

On/off switch

Super-strong suction pads

Fig 393. Fred

Fishing rod with supersonic shoot-out net.

Fig 394.
Sky Dancers

Mechanical fireflies that light up and fly at night. Operated by remote control.

Remote control

Property of Henrig Crumb

Muldoon

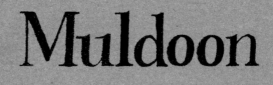

Old stone
barn

Hamish's old
fishing tug

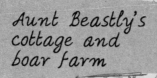

Aunt Beastly's
cottage and
boar farm

Games field

Campsite

Loch Greythorn

Muldoon village

Train station →

Chapter ONE

"**I** am going to catch a monster," said Scarlett. Otto and Martha ignored her.

"I am!" said Scarlett. "You wait and see!"

The Crumbs were on the platform at Sharkstooth Bay train station. They were going with Aunt Beastly to Scotland for a "holiday", to give their dad, Henrig, some time to work on his inventions at home.

Some holiday it's going to be, thought Otto. *On Aunt Beastly's boar farm, teeming with trumping little horrors. There isn't even a TV in the cottage.*

Bessie was their aunt's *real* name. Scarlett had named her Beastly just last week when she had first showed up at their house to look after them. According to Scarlett, the youngest Crumb, who always spoke her mind, Aunt Beastly was a *way* better name for a hairy old busybody!

Otto looked along the platform. There was still no sign of Aunt Beastly. She had thumped away ten minutes ago to ask the station manager if Basil, her baby wild boar, was allowed out of his travel basket on the train.

"Oh dear," gasped Martha, peering around. "What if Aunt Beastly's been squished by a train?"

Martha, who was almost eleven, said things like this all the time. She was terrified of *many* things, but especially of deadly things happening to her family.

Henrig, their father, patted Martha's arm. "Don't worry," he said. "I'm sure she'll be back any minute now."

"Yeah," tutted Scarlett under her breath. "Worse luck." Scarlett tossed back her wild red curls and gave Otto a pinch.

"Ow!"

"So, what's with the bird?" she giggled.

Otto frowned. "It's a lookout device. Dad made it."

Henrig Crumb was a great inventor. But

12

after his wife, Clarice, had died last year he hadn't felt like doing much. It was only recently that the mountain of unpaid bills had forced him to dust down his inventing room and start working again.

Henrig's last invention was an unbreakable glass case to guard a priceless golden elephant on display in the local museum. But he also made more normal, everyday objects to help around the house, as well as toys and gadgets for his children. They were taking some of these with them on their holiday...

Otto, a skinny nine-year-old, had brought **Zac**, his **Z**ip-**A**ctivated **C**amouflage tent (which disappeared at the pull of a zip!) and his new spy-bird, Squawk. Otto wanted to be a detective like his TV hero, Montague Plum, and he hoped to get in some practice during this trip.

Squawk, he knew, would not disappoint, for he was no *ordinary* bird but an ingenious creation of bolts and springs. Not only could he fly really high but he could also tail "suspects" from the air. A video camera on Squawk's tummy would beam footage back to Otto's watch, so he could keep an eye on anyone he liked!

Scarlett was six and three-quarters, and a tomboy through and through. She was taking **Fred**, an invention that looked like an ordinary fishing rod but, on the flick of a switch, shot out a huge net that was hidden inside.

Scarlett had heard that monsters lurked in the lochs of the Scottish Highlands and she planned to use Fred to capture one. That would show her friends what *real* pets were like!

Scarlett was actually wearing the other

invention she was taking on holiday – her **Creeper-Sneakers**. Henrig had modified an ordinary pair of trainers so that Scarlett could walk up things – walls and tree trunks, for instance. She could even hang upside down from thick branches like a bat, which was perfect for playing tricks on unsuspecting passers-by!

Martha's gadgets weren't nearly as daring as her younger brother or sister's. Martha was taking her **Sky Dancers** – remote-controlled fireflies that gracefully danced in the night sky, and a life-jacket named **Pod**.

Henrig had made Pod a few years ago because Martha was nervous about going to the beach. But Pod was no ordinary lifejacket – it included a special cord. If you pulled it, Pod would blow up into a giant transparent ball. And inside the ball would be Martha!

Martha liked being inside the big ball – it made her feel very safe. And ever since the Crumb children had bravely stopped some notorious robbers (called the Unstoppables) stealing the golden elephant from the museum last week, she'd been wearing Pod nearly all the time. She'd been pulling the cord an awful lot, too.

Otto checked his watch again. Their train was coming soon. "I'm sending Squawk to track down Aunt Beastly," he said.

He pressed the tracker button on his watch. The little bird flapped its wings then fluttered away down the platform.

Otto checked the screen on his watch. He could see the pictures Squawk was beaming back of the people down below.

There was an assortment of men, women and children but no sign of his aunt. She was so big and hairy you couldn't miss her!

After a few moments Squawk rounded a corner and Otto spotted Aunt Beastly instantly. She was standing near a ticket machine and, by the way her arms were waving, it looked like she was having a row with a man in uniform.

"Aunt Beastly located, Dad," said Otto. "But I don't think she's happy. Shall I go and get her before she misses the train?"

"Good idea, Otto!" Henrig replied. "But be quick. The train will be here in a few minutes."

"I will." Otto hurried off to where his aunt was arguing with the station manager. Three old men were standing by, watching the quarrel.

Otto stopped a little way off and a chirruping Squawk landed softly on his shoulder.

"Well done, Squawk," Otto whispered. "A very successful first mission!"

Aunt Beastly sounded crosser than ever...

"But Basil is a very rare tufty-tailed boar!" she bellowed at the top of her voice.

"*Well, I don't care!*" the station manager puffed back, glaring at Basil in Aunt Beastly's travel case.

"Rules are rules and that ... that ... *thing* must stay in his basket ALL the way to Muldoon!"

"*But that's nearly the whole day!*" Aunt Beastly roared. "He'll need to stretch his legs!"

"Too bad," sniffed the guard. "And if you don't like it, you know what you can do!" He turned his back and marched away.

"Oooh!" Aunt Beastly looked fit to explode. "*PREPOSTEROUS!*"

Otto saw her cheeks turn post-box red and her hairy nostrils flare out. She was completely bonkers when it came to wild boars, and especially bonkers about Basil.

Otto hurried over to his aunt. "Our train is about to arrive," he said.

"All right! All right!" Aunt Beastly barked, looking very hot and bothered. She bustled away. "Come on then! Hurry up!"

The three old men watched them go. They were standing in the queue by the ticket machine, holding ancient, well-worn suitcases.

"Muldoon," whispered the short, fat one with the long white beard.

"That's what she said," sniffed the thin one. His face was lined with deep wrinkles, like a field that had just been ploughed.

"Hmmm," wheezed the third man in the grey tweed coat and matching hat.

He waited until they were quite alone, then stood up straight and suddenly didn't seem doddery at all. "Right!" he snapped in a completely different voice that sounded much younger and sterner. "Lenny! Doug! Get us three tickets to Muldoon!"

Sebastian Stinkerton pulled off his tweed cap and scratched under his silver-grey wig. The Unstoppables might be masters of disguise but this wig was incredibly itchy!

The robbers had been tailing the Crumbs all week, ever since the kids had spectacularly wrecked their plan of stealing the priceless golden elephant from the Sharkstooth Bay Museum.

Stinkerton had left the museum with nothing, and he couldn't *bear* this feeling of failure. He NEVER failed!

And as if *that* wasn't bad enough, he was convinced that the littlest freckly Crumb girl had even had the nerve to steal something of *his*! It was his top-secret scrapbook. Inside it were photographs and notes on *all* the robberies he'd ever done. It *even* had photos of Stinkerton without his disguises!

If this book ever got into the wrong hands

– the hands of the police, for instance – they'd have enough evidence to lock the Unstoppables in jail for a very long time.

The last time Stinkerton remembered having the book was during the museum job. And the only explanation he could think of was that the red-headed girl had swiped it then. He had to get it back.

"Hey, gov," whispered Lenny. "We've got the tickets."

"Come on then," said Stinkerton. "To the train!"

They hurried off to the platform.

"And remember to act like old men!" Stinkerton hissed.

Stinkerton knew only too well that his sidekicks were unreliable. When they weren't in disguise, Doug was short, fat and bald. He was only good for scoffing crisps, although he did sometimes pass on tip-offs for new robberies from his dodgy mates.

Tall, thin Lenny constantly bickered with Doug, but he was useful because he had a photographic memory. Lenny could memorize the layout of a building in seconds – he knew where everything was, including the niftiest getaway routes and how to get to the treasures.

"Right," whispered Stinkerton as the Crumbs came into view. "Don't let those pesky kids out of your sight!"

Chapter TWO

The train hissed to a stop at the platform. Aunt Beastly hugged Henrig, nearly squashing him flat.

"Well," Henrig gasped, as he struggled to get his breath back. "Have a safe trip, everyone!"

"I wish you could come too, Dad," said Martha.

"I know." Henrig nodded. "I'll miss you so much. You just have fun with your aunt in Scotland!"

Otto, Martha and Scarlett exchanged glances. *Fat chance.*

The children hugged their dad and boarded the train. Aunt Beastly found them seats around a table and they waved to Henrig through the window as the train moved off.

Aunt Beastly popped Basil's basket on the table and Scarlett got out a few travel games.

They began to play Cluedo, which was Otto's favourite, but their aunt seemed determined to tell them about Muldoon...

"There's a grumpy old fisherman called Hamish McTavy," she said, "who lives on a boat in the loch. And there are mists and rainstorms like you've never seen!"

"Oh," sighed Otto. Rainstorms sounded dull!

Aunt Beastly then told them how she'd come to live there, even though they'd already heard the story. She'd moved there recently from India, where she'd spent *years* trying to track down a species called the tufty-tailed boar. It was just like a normal boar, but with a big tufty tail.

The rest of the world had long thought that tufty-tailed boars were extinct. Aunt Beastly, though, was sure that they were not. While she was in India, she had met a couple called Mora and Barry Stewart, who happened to be there on holiday. They had told Aunt Beastly that they, too, thought tufty-tailed boars *did* exist. They said they were sure they'd even *seen* some in the village where they lived – Muldoon, in Scotland.

So Aunt Beastly had bought an old cottage near Loch Greythorn, in Muldoon, and moved there a few months ago. She planned to start a tufty-tailed boar farm, so she'd bought a few baby boars – including her favourite, Basil – in the hope that some of their tails might turn tufty. She had hired a farm hand, too, called Donald McDonald.

While Aunt Beastly was visiting the Crumbs, she'd instructed Donald to buy three more baby boars and settle them in. But Donald had phoned the Crumbs' house yesterday begging Aunt Beastly to come home. He had told her he needed help, but he wouldn't explain why. And

he had sounded ever so flustered.

Aunt Beastly had finally agreed to return home and it was decided that the children would go, too.

"I shall need lots of help on the farm!" said Aunt Beastly. "Mucking out the boars and such like."

The children suddenly sat bolt upright and their eyes grew wide.

"I th-think I'm allergic to b-boars!" gasped Martha. "And I'm *definitely* allergic to boar poop."

"Yep, me too!" Scarlett grinned.

"And I wanted to do other things," Otto said. "Like solve new crimes and stuff."

Aunt Beastly frowned. "Crimes!" she snapped. "Oh no – we had enough of all that last week!" She sniffed. "No more crime-solving, thank you. But there'll be plenty of other things to do. With those three new boars that Donald's bought, there'll be *ten* altogether. Why, their tails might tuft at any second. We must check their bottoms every day!"

As the train chuffed on through sunshine and rain, the Unstoppables were sitting a few seats behind the Crumbs, watching them like hawks. If Stinkerton could just catch a glimpse of his scrapbook in the freckly kid's hands, he could make his move.

"I'm hungry," Doug moaned across the table.

"Quiet!" Stinkerton hissed.

"What if she's left the book at home?" groaned Lenny.

"Why bother stealing it just to leave it at home!" snapped Stinkerton.

Lenny scratched his face. "This stupid

wrinkle paint's bringing me out in spots."

"Stop whinging!"

Then suddenly they heard the littlest Crumb complain loudly that she was starving.

Stinkerton glowered at Doug. "She's just like you!" He saw the hairy aunt wriggle to her feet. "What a walrus of a woman she is," he muttered, watching her head down the aisle towards the buffet car.

Stinkerton sat up and his sly eyes twinkled. The children were all alone. If the freckly kid *did* have his book, now would be the perfect time to get it back.

He watched as the kid unzipped her rucksack.

"Brought any toffees?" her brother asked, but the red-headed Crumb just grinned.

She rummaged in her bag and whipped out, not a toffee, but – Stinkerton gasped...

"My scrapbook!"

Stinkerton heard the oldest girl ask what exactly it was. He clenched his fists as the flame-headed little thief boasted how she'd got it the night of the robbery and how it used to belong to the leader of the Unstoppables but now it was *hers*.

He could hardly bear to watch as the meddlesome kids rifled through the pages. All those photos of *him*. Even some without his disguises! As well as plans for every robbery the Unstoppables had ever done.

"Shall I go and get it back?" asked Lenny.

"Not yet," replied Stinkerton. "We're coming up to a station. We need to wait until then, so we can make a swift getaway. And *I* will get it back, not you!"

"Whoa!" gasped Otto, as page after page gave away more and more secrets. Montague Plum would give his right arm for evidence like this!

"But," Martha whispered, "d-don't you know what this means? Now the Unstoppables will be after us! They're bound to want to get the book back – this is more than enough evidence to send them to jail forever. We're *doomed*!"

Immediately she pulled Pod's cord and the life jacket exploded into a giant transparent ball. In the middle of this ball was a worried-looking Martha. The table had got in the way and the ball was all squashed up. What if it popped? Pod would be wrecked!

"Eeek!" squeaked Martha. She pulled the cord again and Pod returned to a normal life jacket.

Scarlett shook her head. "You're weird."

Otto checked the coast was clear then whispered to his sisters. "The photos in this scrapbook will help the police find the robbers. Then the evidence inside it will send them to jail for life!"

"Who says I'm giving it to the police?" scowled Scarlett. "I'm keeping it to show my friends!"

She stuffed the book back into her rucksack and placed it on the table as the train began to slow down at Kippersfield Station.

"You can't keep the book," Otto frowned.

"Can too!" replied Scarlett stubbornly.

All of a sudden, Scarlett's rucksack was gone. One minute it was there, the next an old man was sprinting off down the aisle with it.

Scarlett leaped to her feet. "Thief!" she shouted. "Stop him!"

At that moment, the carriage door opened and Aunt Beastly appeared carrying a bag of sandwiches. Her enormous body blocked the doorway.

"Out of the way, woman!" Stinkerton snarled.

"How *dare* you!" boomed Aunt Beastly. "No one speaks to me like that, not even an old man!"

Then she noticed Scarlett's rucksack clutched tightly in his hands and heard the children's shouts of, "*Stop him!*"

"Hey!" yelled Aunt Beastly. She threw out an arm and wrenched the rucksack from his grip.

"No!" roared Stinkerton, making a dive for it.

But Aunt Beastly was too quick for him – she brought the bag of sandwiches down on his grey tweed hat. "Take that, you rude old man!"

The sandwich bag split with a loud *r-r-i-i-p!* and soggy tomatoes and lettuce leaves rained down on Stinkerton's shoulders.

"You great galumphing walrus!" he spluttered, as a splodge of gloopy mayonnaise went sliding down his nose. He barged his way past Aunt Beastly as the train came to a stop.

"Yes! Get out of here!" Aunt Beastly roared after him. "And don't you ever come back, do you hear me!"

The children tried to get down the aisle to their aunt but a line of passengers getting off at

Kippersfield blocked the way. Otto jumped on to a seat to see what was going on.

"Don't worry, children!" Aunt Beastly called. "I've got Scarlett's bag back and the nasty thief's gone. Don't panic!"

Once the aisle had emptied, Aunt Beastly arrived back at her seat. "What a horrid old man!" she puffed, handing Scarlett her rucksack.

"Are you awfully wounded? Will you die?" asked Martha.

"No, no," said Aunt Beastly. "I'm built of sturdy stuff, you know! But that nasty thief ruined our sandwiches. Urgh!"

Otto was peering out of the window. If he could get a glimpse of the robber's face he could make "Wanted" posters like Plum did in *The Case of the Great Train Robbery*.

The robber had been wearing a grey tweed

coat and a matching hat. Otto scanned the platform, trying to spot someone fitting that description. But there were so many people about it was hopeless.

Then suddenly he glimpsed a grey tweed hat in amongst the sea of heads. That was him! But wait a minute...

Otto narrowed his eyes. The robber wasn't alone. There were two other old men with him. They were huddled together in conversation.

"Hey!" gasped Otto. He was pretty sure these three old men were the ones he'd glimpsed by the ticket machine back at Sharkstooth Bay Station.

Otto's brain began to whirr. He tried to imagine the three old guys without the white hair and wrinkles. One of them was short and fat. The other was tall and thin. And the third – the one who'd tried to steal Scarlett's rucksack

– looked much wiser than the others.

Otto wondered if his thick white moustache was, in fact, a *false* one. He wondered if underneath it there was a real, dark brown one? Could this be ... Sebastian Stinkerton?

"Whoa!" breathed Otto, as it dawned on him. These three old men weren't *old* at all. They were in disguise. *The Unstoppables!*

Aunt Beastly had managed to stop them this time, but if they'd tried to steal Scarlett's rucksack, that meant they *knew* she had the scrapbook. Otto was sure it wouldn't be the last he saw of them.

He whipped out his Solving Crimes Notebook and scribbled down a new heading:

Case 432: Stopping the Unstoppables (for good!)

Chapter THREE

As the train sped on, further and further north, Otto couldn't stop thinking about the Unstoppables. He knew they'd go to any lengths to get the scrapbook back, and he'd already seen how cunning they could be.

"What if that robber had tried to steal *Basil*!" ranted Aunt Beastly. "Really, whatever next!"

It was clear that she had no idea *who* this thief really was. Otto was certain his sisters hadn't twigged either.

But should he *tell* them? If he did, his aunt would certainly want to take over, Martha would panic like mad and Scarlett would pout because he'd blown her secret about the scrapbook.

Otto gazed out of the window, trying to decide what to do. His aunt was cross enough about the robber already.

She began to tell them a story about how,

when she was Scarlett's age, a beastly girl at school had stolen something from her, too...

"It was this lovely blue crayon," she said. "No one else in my class had one like it. The most perfect colour for sky you'd ever seen! So I kept it hidden right at the bottom of my gym bag. Then one day Belinda Strawbottom *stole* it. I found it in her desk before class the next morning. So I took it back then glued her desk shut with a half-chewed toffee!"

"Cool!" cried Scarlett. She'd have done the same. In fact, she'd have to remember that toffee trick.

Thinking of toffee made Scarlett's tummy rumble. They still hadn't eaten anything.

"I need food," she wailed. "I'm starving!"

"But I don't want to leave you again," said Aunt Beastly. "Not after what's just happened."

"The robber's gone," replied Otto. "We'll be fine."

He'd decided to tell his sisters about the Unstoppables. He wasn't sure about his aunt just yet. If she knew *those* robbers were back, her ranting would probably get them all thrown off the train!

"Oh, I *wish* I'd brought cabbage sandwiches, now," Aunt Beastly said with a sigh. "I don't know *where* that cabbage I bought yesterday went to!"

The children did. They had chucked it in the bin so that they could eat something *other* than cabbage for once.

"For cabbage," Aunt Beastly droned on, "is what makes children strong and healthy! My trusty old book says just that. But the buffet car doesn't do cabbage anything!"

44

"Shame," tutted Scarlett, hiding a smirk. "Can we have sausage sandwiches instead then?"

"Just this once?" Otto pleaded.

"Please?" Martha begged.

Aunt Beastly stood up. "Well, mind you look after Basil!"

As soon as she'd gone, Otto whispered, "That guy who tried to steal Scarlett's rucksack... He was Sebastian Stinkerton, leader of the Unstoppables."

"No!" Martha quivered and rummaged around in her pockets for fluff. Martha always made good-luck charms out of fluff in times of great danger. "This calls for lucky-fluffles!" she cried. "Are you *sure* it was him?"

"Yep," Otto nodded. "I saw his gang with him on the platform. They were huddled together, talking."

"But how do you know it was them?" frowned Scarlett. "You always think the worst, Otto."

"That's the job of a detective," Otto replied.

"But you're *not* a detective!" scowled Scarlett.

"Listen," Otto said, "the Unstoppables are definitely after that scrapbook. We might have shaken them off for now but they'll be back. What we need is a really good plan."

"We're doomed!" cried Martha. She abandoned her fluff and reached for Pod's cord.

"Wait, Martha!" cried Otto. "We need your help with the plan!"

Martha stopped and thought for a moment. "O-okay."

"Anyway, *I'm* not scared," sniffed Scarlett, her freckly nose in the air. "It's them who should be scared of *me*. They know I can pinch like a crab!"

"Yeah, but last time they got away," said Otto.

"This time we have to put them in jail. We've got to hand that scrapbook over to the police as soon as we get to Scotland. Do you think we should tell Aunt Beastly, or not?"

He'd feel really bad if he didn't because she'd helped during the museum robbery. On that night they'd felt like a real team.

"I-I think we *should* tell her," Martha nodded.

"No way!" cried Scarlett. "She'll make me hand the book over!"

"But you can't keep the book, whatever we do," said Otto.

Otto thought hard. Their aunt, with her giant muscles, would be a big help. And they'd need all the help they could get to put those robbers in jail.

"Let's tell her," he said at last. "But maybe when she's calmed down a bit."

"Do it when we get off the train," said Martha.

"Hmmm," Otto nodded. "Good idea."

When Aunt Beastly returned she *did* have sausage sandwiches. Otto closed his eyes as he bit into his. It was *bliss*.

"Just this once, mind!" sniffed Aunt Beastly. "As a treat for Scarlett, who must be *awfully* scared after that nasty old robber snatched her bag."

Scarlett nodded solemnly, trying her best not to grin. "I am," she sighed. "I am *so, so* scared that I might need ketchup, too ... and maybe

chips with salt and vinegar?"

"Absolutely not!" replied Aunt Beastly.

As the train chuffed on, Otto observed the passengers carefully. He noticed something strange. The closer they got to Scotland, the more weird and wonderful the people joining the train became. All sorts that you wouldn't normally expect...

A man down the aisle was making paper sculptures of tall skyscrapers and fancy bridges. Further along, two women were arranging dried flowers. Some people were knitting funny fruit shapes out of wool, a couple were doing a collage and a strongman was lifting heavy weights.

"Where do you think all these people are going?" Otto asked his aunt.

"Oh, I expect they're off to Muldoon!"

HIGHLANDS FLYER

"But that's where *we're* going," Martha said.

"Why are they going there?" asked Scarlett.

"Probably for the Highland Games," said Aunt Beastly. "The locals tell me there are Games held every year in the field on the other side of the loch to my cottage. They start in two days' time – this Wednesday – and go on for three days. But I didn't think you'd be interested

50

HIGHLANDS 🌿 FLYER

in anything like that."

"Course we are!" Scarlett cried. The prospect of any kind of "games" sounded *way* more fun than shovelling up stinky boar poop all day!

"So, what happens?" Otto asked. Then he immediately wished he hadn't.

"Well," said Aunt Beastly. "I'll tell you *all* about it! Now, let's see..."

She settled herself back in her seat and proceeded to tell them the history of the Games – from the Dark Ages right up to now.

She told them about all the events there were, including tossing the caber (which was throwing a tree trunk, she said), craft events, hammer throwing with metal balls instead of hammers, Highland dancing and much, much more!

She said that people came from far and wide to compete, and that they took it very seriously.

"But you said you lived in a quiet place," said Otto.

"I do!" Aunt Beastly nodded. "The locals told me when I moved in that nothing ever happens in Muldoon. Except for the Games, that is. The rest of the time it's incredibly quiet, so they said."

In another part of the train, the Unstoppables sat twiddling their thumbs. Before the train had left Kippersfield, they'd sneaked back on further down the platform and got changed into businessmen disguises.

Now they all wore impeccable pinstriped suits, and – instead of carrying big old suitcases – they had very shiny briefcases. Stinkerton even had a neat bowler hat.

Doug yawned behind his newspaper. He was bored, starving hungry and the seats were uncomfortable. "I'm gonna try and get the scrapbook," he muttered. "Then we can get off this train."

"No!" snapped Lenny. "I'll do it. I'm a *way* better robber than you!"

"Shhh!" hissed Stinkerton. "We've gone through this! We have to wait until we get to Muldoon."

"Oh!" came a voice. It was the man across the aisle. The robbers glanced over.

The man had a mass of black curly hair, muscles as big as mountains and an extremely large smile...

"Did you say you're going to *Muldoon*?" he asked in a strong Welsh accent.

"Um..." said Stinkerton.

"Yeah!" cried Doug.

Stinkerton nudged him in the ribs. How many times had he told his sidekicks that it was him, Stinkerton, that always did the talking?

"Not off to the Highland Games by any chance, are you?" asked the muscly man.

"Nnnn—" began Doug, but Stinkerton nudged him again.

"Yes, actually, we are," lied Stinkerton. "We're going to compete."

"Oh, brilliant!" cried the man. "I didn't think you were for a minute because of your very smart suits."

"Er, we always travel smartly!" Stinkerton replied. "We keep our kit in our luggage."

"Oh, yes – absolutely!" replied the muscly Welshman. "I'm Ifor Ramm and I'm a competitor, too. Very pleased to meet you!"

He threw out one of his spade-sized hands and shook each of theirs, almost crushing them.

"Ouch!" winced Lenny.

"Sorry about that." Ifor smiled. "I sometimes forget I have such enormous muscles! Now, I don't like to boast but you'll find out soon enough, so I may as well tell you ... I am a champion caber-tosser. Oh, yes!"

He pointed to a big bunch of medals on his jacket and a rosette the size of a sunflower. Upon it in gold letters were the words *Champ of Champs!*

"And this is my family!" Ifor said with a nod.

He introduced his wife and twin daughters, who all had giant muscles like him. They were sporting huge rosettes saying, *Champ of Champs' Family*.

Some other Highland Games competitors had been listening in on the conversation. They were keen to size up the new competition.

"Have you ever won trophies?" called a bearded Irish man, who looked like a hairy wolfhound.

"What Games have you been at?" a lady asked.

"Are you camping by Loch Greythorn?" said a little boy.

So many questions! This was bad. Stinkerton began to feel edgy. The plan had been to keep a low profile, not draw attention to themselves.

"What event are you doing?" beamed a young Scottish lady, who was holding a set of bagpipes. She puffed into them until she turned purple in the face and a strangled note screeched out. It sounded like someone had sat on a cat.

"Yes, what *are* you doing?" Ifor repeated.

"Er," said Stinkerton. "O-our event's ... really ... rare. You've probably not even heard of it..."

"Highland dancing!" Doug blurted out at the top of his voice. He had seen a documentary about it once – they jumped over swords and everything. How cool was that!

Stinkerton glowered at him. They'd never danced in their *lives*. And now they'd have to skip around looking silly!

Chapter FOUR

T he train trundled into Muldoon and everyone got off. They had arrived, at last!

Out on the platform it was drizzly and cold. "What a dead-end dump," muttered Stinkerton. He looked around, then whispered to the others, "Stay close!"

An eerie mist curled through the air.

"I don't like it here, it's spooky," Doug whispered.

"Don't be such a baby!" Stinkerton hissed.

Suddenly, Stinkerton spotted the Crumbs. They were talking to a dim-looking lad with hair like a messy haystack. Stinkerton wondered if he should make a quick dive for the scrapbook now. He could see the rucksack on the freckly girl's back.

MULDOON

But there were so many people about, he would never manage to escape without attracting attention. Besides, Muldoon station was at the end of the line and there'd be no more trains out of here tonight. No, they'd have to stick to their story for now and follow the competitors to their campsite.

"I wonder where the walrus-woman lives," said Stinkerton, watching the Crumbs through the crowd. He would have to find that out in the morning. Snooping about now would be too obvious, but tomorrow they could ask a few questions. In a small place like this, someone was bound to know.

The Unstoppables followed a stream of people out into a tiny car park. A coach was waiting to take spectators and competitors to their guest houses or the campsite on the banks of Loch Greythorn.

As they queued for the coach, Stinkerton saw the Crumbs climb into a muddy truck. Inside he spotted several little boars, just like the one in the aunt's travel basket. He stroked his neat, bottlebrush moustache. "How revolting!"

The truck clattered off down a bumpy track.

"Hey, gov," said Doug. "We ain't got a tent. What will we sleep in tonight?"

"We'll sort something out," hissed Stinkerton. "Now get on the coach!"

In the truck, Aunt Beastly met the new boars.

"Oh, they're little angels!" she cried. "But why did you need me to come home, Donald? They look just fine to me."

"I..." began Donald, then he quickly changed

the subject. "Och! We've had buckets of rain here, you know!"

Otto got the feeling that Donald was hiding something. Just like *he* was. He thought back to what had happened on the train. He still hadn't told his aunt about the Unstoppables...

"Aunt Bessie," said Otto. "I've got something to tell you."

Suddenly one of the baby boars did a noisy trump. The children wrinkled up their noses as a smell like mouldy cheese filled the air.

"We'll be gassed!" coughed Martha.

"Don't be silly!" barked Aunt Beastly. "And Donald, kindly answer me – why did you need me home? I know you remembered to buy the boars because they're right here, all three of them."

"Aye," muttered Donald. "I bought the boars all right..."

They turned up a track and Otto glimpsed the loch in the headlights as they bumped along. Then Donald pulled up outside an old stone cottage.

"So, Donald – what are you hiding?" barked Aunt Beastly as everyone climbed out. The children were each holding a wriggling boar and Aunt Beastly had Basil nestled under her cavernous armpit. "Spit it out, Donald!" she roared. "Tell me!"

"Och, well..." gulped Donald as they walked towards the cottage. He couldn't put it off any longer. "I remembered you told me to get *some* wee boars but I couldnee remember how many."

"So?" snapped Aunt Beastly. Her piggy eyes narrowed and her cheeks turned bright red.

Donald quivered. "I did write it down like you told me!" he gulped. "But then I ... sort of ... lost my wee note."

He hung his head. "I-I knew it had the number *three* in it but I couldnee remember how *many* threes. I thought maybe ... *two* threes so, um,

that's what I ordered. Then I found my wee note which just said *one* three but by then it was too late, cos the farmer had brought 'em all, see?"

Aunt Beastly reeled. She didn't *see* at all. "Two threes ... one three ... a note...? Hang on," she said finally, her thick nostril hair twitching. "Don't tell me you bought ... *thirty-three* boars? We don't have room for thirty-three! My goodness – just where have you *put* them all, man?"

There was silence as deep as falling snow. Donald's eyes flicked from Aunt Beastly to the tiny stone cottage.

"No!" boomed Aunt Beastly. "They'll never all fit in there!"

She thundered up to the cottage door, edged it open and they all peeped inside.

"Eee—" squeaked Aunt Beastly, stepping back again in horror. There were boars...

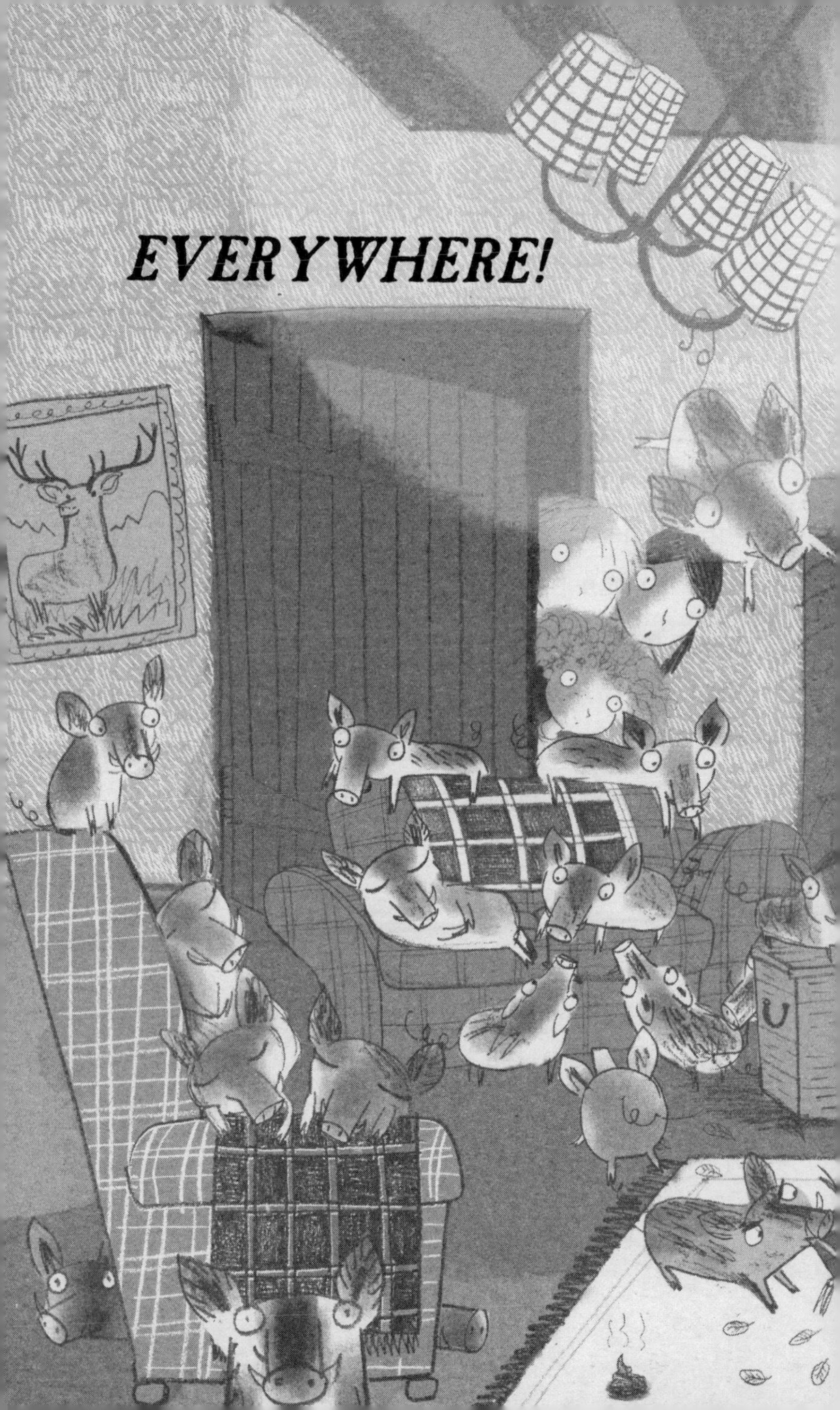
EVERYWHERE!

The children squeezed in and put down the wriggly boars they were holding.

Aunt Beastly looked stunned. She was lost for words. Gaping, she shuffled in, too.

Donald followed, closing the door behind them. He hung back as Aunt Beastly and the children peered round the living room. It was jam-packed with leaping, ripping, gnawing and trumping little boars.

For a moment Aunt Beastly just stood there, her face like a great wet haddock. Then she shook herself, put down Basil and grunted, "Right!"

She bulldozed forward, stepping over boars as she went. Otto and Martha followed, but Scarlett took a different route – up a wall then across the ceiling. Her gravity-defying Creeper-Sneakers were amazing!

It wasn't long before they discovered that the boars had got upstairs, too.

"There are boars in the bath!" Scarlett cried.

"A-and in the beds!" Martha mumbled.

"They're under them, too!" Otto pointed a finger. "And in the wardrobes and the cupboards and the drawers. Look – there's even one in the loo!"

"Urrggghh!" the children shuddered. "Gross!"

"DONALD!" Aunt Beastly bellowed.

But Donald, it seemed, had crept away.

"Right!" Aunt Beastly barked again, sounding like she really meant business. "First thing in the morning I shall call that farmer who dumped all these boars in my house and *insist* he takes the other thirty back. No way will any of their tails tuft with them crammed in like sardines!"

Aunt Beastly's eyes flicked to the children.

"Bed!" she snapped. "All of you. Have you *seen* how late it is?"

"But the *boars* are in our beds!" Scarlett giggled.

"And there's mud on the pillows!" shrieked Martha.

"Aunt Bessie," said Otto. "I've brought my tent. Couldn't we all sleep in that?"

"What, *all* of us?" Aunt Beastly cried, grabbing some pillows and blankets.

"Not you!" gasped Scarlett. Her brother's tent was a pop-up one. It would be more like a *blow-up* one if Aunt Beastly tried to squeeze her enormous backside in!

"Scarlett means," said Otto, "you should stay here to, um, read the boars a bedtime story! They'd probably be scared if you left them on their own."

"Oh, go on then – off you all go! But mind you put the tent right next to the house, and no wandering round outside!"

"Okay!" Otto smiled. He nudged his sisters and grabbed some bedding from their aunt. Then, snatching up their rucksacks, they hurried out into the garden.

Otto unpacked the tent, they popped it up and his sisters crawled sleepily inside. He was just about to follow when he noticed something on the other side of the loch.

There were lots of little lights in the opposite field coming from torches and smouldering campfires.

"Oh! The Highland Games camp!" he said.

In the middle of the camp there looked to be a big white marquee with a smaller one right beside it. To the left of these was a huge field, to the right were rows and rows of tents.

It would be easy for the Unstoppables to hide out among all those people, thought Otto.

Before going to sleep, he took the robbers' scrapbook from Scarlett's rucksack and popped it under his pillow.

"Hey, what are you doing?" Scarlett frowned.

"Keeping the book really close," replied Otto.

He was sure the Unstoppables wouldn't give up on the scrapbook that easily...

E arly next morning a watery sun rose over the tiny village of Muldoon. Birds were twittering in the trees and a thick white mist crept low over the loch.

The Highland Games competitors were still fast asleep. All except one – Sebastian Stinkerton. The leader of the Unstoppables hadn't had a wink of sleep all night.

When the robbers had arrived at the field last night there was only one tent left for hire. It was a tatty, leaky green one that smelled of cat wee and mould. They'd been forced to take it – and even pay for it! – because that's what Games competitors *would* do, and if Stinkerton wanted to get his scrapbook back, he couldn't do anything to risk blowing their cover.

But for Stinkerton, trying to sleep in a whiffy old tent was totally impossible. Especially with

Doug's growly snores and Lenny's bony elbows poking him in the back.

"Oi! You two," Stinkerton snarled. "Come on! Wake up – it's morning."

He wafted Doug's shoe under Lenny's nose.

"Bleuch!" heaved Lenny, coughing awake. "Wassat? It's revolting!"

"Your breakfast!" snapped Stinkerton sarcastically, prodding Doug's enormous tummy. "Get up! You need to go to the camp shop and buy us our new disguises."

"Buy them? Not nick them?"

"No!" barked Stinkerton. "We can't do anything to risk getting caught, remember?"

Lenny and dumpy Doug sat up. They still wore yesterday's suits, though they were now looking very crumpled indeed.

"Go and get us some kilts and, and ... all the

other bits that go with them," ordered Stinkerton.

"Like what?" yawned Doug.

"Like everything we'll need!"

Lenny and Doug rubbed their eyes and crawled sleepily out of the tent.

"And don't come back without all the right gear, or else," Stinkerton called after them.

While they were gone, Stinkerton worked out a simple plan to get his book back. They just needed to find out where that walrus-woman lived, then get over there and hunt for the scrapbook.

Eventually, Doug and Lenny came back with a pile of Highland dancing gear.

"Look, we've got everything!" Doug beamed.

They changed into itchy kilts, itchy shirts, itchy knee-length socks and itchy hats with big fluffy pom-poms on!

Lenny looked down at himself in disgust. "Stupid draughty skirt!" he scowled. "My botty's flipping freezing!"

"It's not a skirt, it's a *kilt*," smiled Doug. "And I really like it! It even comes with a guinea pig attached! Look!" He pointed to the funny furry thing dangling down the front of his kilt.

"That's your *sporran*!" Stinkerton sighed. "It's a Scottish man-purse."

"Wow!" giggled Doug. "Somewhere to keep our stolen money!"

Lenny glowered. "I am *not* going out in this!"

"Yes, you are," said Stinkerton coolly. "Because *this* is what Highland dancers wear! Now we've got to get out and practise, while we try and find out where that boar farm is."

"P-practise!" spluttered Lenny. "What ... skipping around? We're going to look like idiots!"

"Well, you two should feel right at home then!" snapped Stinkerton. "Come on!"

Out in the campsite, a number of competitors were already up and walking about.

"I hate this stupid skirt," grumbled Lenny.

"Concentrate, will you!" Stinkerton growled. "May I remind you how important it is we get

my scrapbook off those kids. If we don't, it could land us in jail forever!"

"All right! All right!" Lenny muttered. "I get it!"

The Unstoppables walked across the camping field and through a gate in the willow-cane fence that led to the competition area. They now found themselves in a huge field split up into smaller areas by thick hay-bale walls. Each area had a sign listing the events taking place there.

The very first area the Unstoppables came to was the Highland dancing. Some competitors were already practising on the stage and others were running through their routines in groups.

"I am *not* skipping!" Lenny sniffed.

"You will!" boomed Stinkerton. "Otherwise we'll blow our cover. Idiot!"

They had a quick practice, which went very badly, as Doug and Lenny had two left feet.

Then they walked along to the caber-tossing field to see if someone there might have heard mention of the boar farm.

A group of muscly men and women were throwing huge tree trunks through the air. Doug waved to Ifor, the man they'd met on the train.

"Hi!" called Ifor, waving back while balancing a tree trunk in his other spade-sized hand. "Watch me throw this. I don't like to boast but honestly, I'm nothing short of amazing!"

The Unstoppables watched. Then they chatted to the caber-tossers and tried to ask casual questions about Muldoon – particularly about *boar farms* in Muldoon. These hints, however, were met with blank looks.

"Nah," said Ifor, shaking his head. "We don't know about that. Anyway, boys, I think sheep are much better than boars!"

Sighing, the Unstoppables moved on. In the next field along, five stone-putters were hurling massive rocks through the air. But they knew nothing about the boar farm either.

Then they spotted the woman bagpiper from the train, but she was busy playing a tune.

"Nice tune!" called Doug, as she went purple in the face.

"It sounds like an exploding toad," said Stinkerton coolly.

The Unstoppables passed a big white marquee with a sign saying "Craft Tent". People were bustling in and out, preparing the displays before the Games started tomorrow.

Next door to the marquee was the food tent.

"Hey, look! It's open for breakfast!" cried Doug, as the smell of sausage, eggs and beans wafted out to meet them.

"No!" snapped Stinkerton. "We can't get distracted. We need to find out where that boar farm is!"

"But—" muttered Doug.

"Keep up!" said Stinkerton, marching off.

He'd only taken a few steps when he spied a very old lady carrying a sign out of the food tent. She placed it on the grass and bustled back in.

Stinkerton read the sign.

Mary McNab's Homemade Delights.

"Mmmm…" said Stinkerton, thinking hard. The old woman probably came from Muldoon – it would be the locals, most likely, who were running the Games. If anyone knew about the boar farm, she would.

"Right then, boys," Stinkerton said. "Let's go and try that food tent after all."

"Ooo! Are we going for breakfast?" beamed Doug.

"No," growled Stinkerton. "We're going for *information*."

He peeped in through the open tent flap. Behind a long counter, he spotted the old lady. This, Stinkerton guessed, must be Mary McNab.

Mary had very wispy white hair that drifted from her head like candle smoke. Her face was etched with deep wrinkles but her stare was as piercing as an eagle's. She wore a shawl and a crisp white linen apron that was spotless.

Stinkerton strode up to the counter with Lenny and Doug behind.

"Aye?" said Mary, raising an eyebrow.

Doug thought she looked just like a witch. On the other hand, her cupcakes looked simply *delicious...*

"What will yer be 'aving then?" Mary asked.

Doug put his hand out and grabbed a large cupcake.

SLAP!

Mary McNab walloped his hand.

Doug dropped the cupcake at once and blushed. "I'm very s-s-sorry!" he squeaked.

"So ye should be!" Mary snapped. Her eagle-eyes narrowed. "Ye *pays* first and eats *later*, yer pigwig!"

"I'm so sorry about my friend," said Stinkerton. "He forgets his manners sometimes. What delightful oatcakes you have there. I'll take three!" In his most charming voice, he added, "And I bet you made them all yourself?"

"Aye," Mary nodded. "But me recipe's top secret."

"Quite right!" Stinkerton flashed her his smarmiest smile. "And am I also right in thinking that you're a local in this pretty village?"

"Aye," Mary nodded. "Lived here all me life."

"Gosh," beamed Stinkerton. "How lovely! I expect you've seen many changes over the years?"

"Well, aye," said Mary, her voice a little warmer now.

Stinkerton waited. He was good at getting people to spill the beans. He nodded and smiled.

Then Mary spoke again. "Aye, I've seen folk come and go. I've seen changes round 'ere, all right."

"And are you a ... farmer?" Stinkerton asked. "Do you grow all the oats for your oatcakes?"

"No, I'm no farmer!" Mary sniffed. "I couldn't be doing with all that. Noise and muck, muck and noise! Like that new boar farm – what a stink! You can even smell it here, though it's on the other side of the loch!"

"The loch?"

"The loch right outside!" tutted Mary. "The new boar farm's on the other side. Bessie Crumb's gone an' got a whole *herd* of stinky boars. The batty old fruitcake!"

Stinkerton grinned. He'd done it! Now he knew where the boar farm was. It would be dead easy to cross the loch in the rowing boats the locals used. The scrapbook was as good as his again!

Aunt Beastly had been up since the crack of dawn examining all the new boars. Before she phoned the farmer to demand he took some back, she thought it wise to check their tails for tuftiness.

She was in the kitchen rescuing Basil from a

jar of honey he'd somehow got all over himself
when the children trooped inside for breakfast.

The house was a complete tip. The boars
had ripped it to shreds! Not that Aunt Beastly
seemed to care any more. She was thinking of
boars and nothing else.

"D-do you think any tails might tuft?" asked
Martha.

"Why, yes!" beamed Aunt Beastly. "All of
them!"

The children looked unconvinced. Every
single tail on every single boar was limp, thin
and bare.

"I've had a change of plan!" Aunt Beastly's
eyes twinkled. "I am going to keep *all* the little
darlings!"

"But where will they live?" Scarlett demanded.
She wrinkled up her nose.

"Well," said Aunt Beastly, popping Basil in the sink to wash his sticky trotters. "We must make them all *pens* to live in! I'm going to ask some villagers to lend a hand. A pen-making party, that's what we'll have. Just the ticket!"

This was *not* what Otto wanted to hear. The last thing he needed was for his day to be taken up with building silly pens when he desperately needed to get that scrapbook to the police.

He would have to tell his aunt about the scrapbook now. And this time he just had to *say* it. He couldn't bottle out like before.

Otto took a deep breath. "Aunt Bessie, I've been trying to te—"

"Hush!" roared Aunt Beastly. "What's that noise? Basil! Oh, goodness – he's choking!"

The wheezy, cross-eyed little boar was foaming at the mouth!

"Do something! Do something!" Aunt Beastly wailed.

"Leave it to me!" said Scarlett.

She rolled up her sleeves then shot out an arm and karate-chopped Basil on the back.

The little boar gave a gurgly cough but nothing came out.

"Again!" roared Aunt Beastly.

Scarlett repeated the action, but harder this time and with a wicked grin on her face.

"Oh!" cried Aunt Beastly. "I think something's happening..."

"*Plaahhh!*" coughed Basil. "*Plaahhh!*"

A large green bar of soap shot out of Basil's mouth, complete with a torrent of lime-coloured bubbles.

"Oh, thank goodness!" Aunt Beastly cried, planting a huge kiss on Basil's head. "No more eating soap, you silly-billy!"

Now that the choking panic was over, Otto tried to mention the scrapbook again.

"Aunt Bessie," he said. "We've got this bo—"

"Oh," boomed Aunt Beastly as Donald sloped in looking very nervous indeed. "You've decided to show your face again, have you?"

As Donald's cheeks turned very red, Otto sighed a big sigh. It was clear his aunt's mind was on other things, but all he could think about was the scrapbook and how to get it to the police right now.

"Aunt Bessie," said Otto, "About making those pens... While you see if the neighbours will help, me and my sisters could ask in the village."

"Really, dear? You'd do that for me?"

Suddenly a boar fight erupted on the stairs and Aunt Beastly thumped off to sort it out.

As soon as she'd gone, Scarlett pinched Otto. "I will *not* troop around asking for silly helpers!"

"We're not," whispered Otto. "I only said that as a cover story – so that we can take the scrapbook to the police."

"I don't want to do that either," hissed Scarlett. "I want that book to show my friends!"

"You can't," gulped Martha. "Otto's right, we have to get it to the police before the robbers get to *us*!"

Scarlett stamped her foot, her face like thunder. "Spoilsports!"

As they ate breakfast, Aunt Beastly turned to Donald, who was shovelling up boar poop off the sofa.

"Anyway, Donald," she said, in a much more cheery voice, "I've actually decided to keep all the boars. For those dear little tails," she said, nodding at the boars, "will be tufting *any minute now*, I'm sure!"

She wolfed down her cabbage on toast then gave a deep burp. "Oops, pardon me! Now, where's my handbag? I need to comb Basil's hair, then get off to the neighbours right away and enlist volunteers to build those boar pens!"

Finally, Aunt Beastly found her bag between the tusks of two snorting, growling boars. "Oh, look – they're playing tug-of-war. Little angels!"

Patting their heads, she tried to take the bag back but the boars held on tight, snarling.

"Give it to Mummy!" Aunt Beastly tittered. It took quite a bit of force to get it but she triumphed in the end.

"Thank you, my precious darlings!" she beamed, wiping the boar dribble off the bag with a tea towel. "There we are. No harm done!" She combed Basil's hair and then did her own with the very same comb.

The children shuddered. "Eww!"

"Now, Donald, listen *very* carefully." Aunt Beastly's voice was stern again. "I'm off out, so look after the boars while I'm gone. And I mean it, Donald. No mishaps."

Donald gulped.

"Right," sniffed Aunt Beastly, tucking Basil under her arm. "Off we go!"

As they left the cottage, Aunt Beastly went off in the direction of Mora and Barry's house and the children headed off up the hill to the village. Otto had the scrapbook packed away in his rucksack, out of sight, in case the

Unstoppables happened to be tailing them.

As they walked, Otto glanced across the loch to the Highland Games camp. They could see lots of activity in the fields.

Suddenly a big black crow came swooping low over their heads.

"Caw! Caw! Caw!" Its screams were deafening.

"Arrrgh!" shrieked Martha. "Crows are bad luck! We're doomed!"

She pulled Pod's cord and the ball inflated, rolling back down the hill with a quivering Martha inside it.

"Not again," groaned Otto, as he and Scarlett plodded down after her.

They found Martha in a large clump of purple heather. She was still inside Pod and she looked sickly green. She had never rolled quite so fast!

"Deflate it, Martha," Otto said.

Martha shook her head.

"Crows mean bad luck!" she called. "The Unstoppables – they *have* to be close."

"So what?" said Scarlett. "I've been practising my karate. Hi-yaaa!"

Eventually Martha pulled the cord and Pod deflated with a hiss. But she still looked very worried and stood there chewing her fingernails.

Muldoon was not her sort of place at all. It was dark and drizzly and jam-packed with danger. And she missed Dad and her nice, safe bedroom so much.

Chapter SIX

Stinkerton rapped hard on the cottage door.
"Wait!" gasped Lenny. "What you gonna say?"

"Just let me do the talking," said Stinkerton coolly.

A few seconds later the door was opened a crack by the dim-looking lad they had seen at the train station. He was holding a boar.

"Can I help you?" he asked.

"Why, yes," smirked Stinkerton, "I do believe you can. We are Highland Games competitors but, right now, I'm looking to buy a boar for my dear grandmother's birthday! She has always been smitten with boars, you see, so I thought I could take her one back after the Games. Anyway, we were told you sold them. Is that correct?"

The lad shook his head. "Ouch!" he cried, as the boar he was holding bit his finger. "Not me –

they're Miss Bessie's. And she is wanting to keep 'em all."

"Oh, no!" cried Doug, a little too mournfully. He wiped a pretend tear from his eye.

Stinkerton gave him a sneaky kick, which made him howl even louder.

"He's very fond of my granny," said Stinkerton. "And could you— What is your name?"

"Donald."

"Could you, Donald, call Miss Bessie now? Perhaps I could persuade her to part with one single little boar?"

"There's no one home but me," said Donald.

"Really?" Stinkerton hid a smile. Why, this was even better! He could snoop around the place so much more easily with just one brainless lad about.

At that moment, the little boar in Donald's arms flew from his grip and belted down the garden, squealing and trumping wildly.

"Get him!" cried Donald. "Quick! Help!"

Donald sprinted off after him but, in his haste, forgot to shut the door. A second later, a stampede of little boars rocketed off outside.

"*Wheee! Wheee! Wheee!*" came their joyful little cries, as they pattered off in all directions.

"Och, no!" shrieked Donald. "Miss Bessie will kill me! Catch 'em!"

While Lenny and Doug hurried to help, Stinkerton slipped into the old stone cottage. Now was his chance to get his scrapbook back!

Donald didn't notice a thing. He was far too busy with the boars, who were now digging up flower beds, ripping washing off the line and diving headlong into great muddy puddles.

"Stop!" yelled Donald, dashing this way and that, attempting to use his belt as a lasso.

"Ow!" roared Doug. "One's biting my ankle. Leave off!"

By the time the last of the boars was rounded up and dumped back inside the cottage, Stinkerton had searched the place from top to bottom. But there was no sign of his scrapbook anywhere.

A panting Donald finally shut the door and did a quick boar headcount.

"Thirty-seven ... thirty-eight ... thirty-nine!" he puffed. "Plus little Basil o'course. That makes ... er..." He scratched his head and started to count on his fingers.

"Forty, you i—!" Stinkerton stopped. Keeping cool was tricky when he was seething inside. The meddlesome kids must have taken his scrapbook with them, wherever it was they had gone. What was it about those Crumbs that made him so ... *arrghhh*!

"We'd better be off then!" Stinkerton barked, stomping back outside.

"I hope your granny has a very happy birthday!" called Donald.

The Unstoppables walked on without another word and climbed into the rowing boat.

"No book?" asked Lenny.

"What do you think?" Stinkerton glowered.

When the children arrived at the police station, the place was deserted apart from one policeman who looked very old and doddery. He was attempting to do a jigsaw.

"More sky or a bit of raccoon?" he muttered, squinting at one of the puzzle pieces right in front of his nose. He didn't seem to notice that the children were even there.

"Excuse me," said Otto.

The policeman jumped. "Who's 'at?" he said, peering around. He snatched up the remains of a baguette and brandished it like a truncheon.

"He's as blind as a bat!" Scarlett whispered. "And I think he's a bit deaf, too."

"Great," groaned Otto. "*Just* the person we need to give the book to."

"Are you friend or foe?" muttered the policeman, now jabbing the baguette about.

"Um, f-friend," said Martha nervously.

"Pardon?" said the policeman.

"FRIEND!" Otto shouted. "And we've got something to give you."

"Oh, friends!" beamed the old policeman. "Jolly good!"

"Listen – we've got something for you," said Scarlett. "Some evidence and it's good."

"Never mind that!" the old policeman chuckled. "Just bung it on the table over there. If there still *is* a table over there? My eyes are none too great these days. Anyway, the question is, can you do jigsaws?"

The children peered around for someone else. Surely this man hadn't been left in charge of the whole police station! Otto shook his head. Where were the smart guys like Montague Plum had on his team? Here they were with a piece of evidence that would put the Unstoppables in jail and all this policeman wanted to do was a jigsaw! Well, there was no way they could give the scrapbook to *him*.

Otto read the name on the policeman's badge, then very loudly said, "Um, Constable Batty, I was just wondering, are there any *other* officers about?"

"Och, no!" the old policeman replied. "Don't yer know 'tis the Games, laddie! Potts is manning the craft tent. Pratt is manning the coach park. Pickle and Bumble are sorting out quarrels at the campsite. And Sergeant Fudge is off sick ... nursing his broken toes. I didn't *mean* to run over them!" he added quickly. "It wasn't *my* fault he got in the way when I was parking the police car. My eyesight's not what it used to be – he knows that!"

"Let's get out of here," Scarlett whispered.

"But what about the s-scrapbook?" Martha muttered.

"We'll decide what to do with that later,"

said Otto. "Come on."

The children trooped out and walked on through the village to have a quick look around. At the end of the main street was a small signpost with "Loch Greythorn" on it.

"This way!" said Scarlett, following the sign and heading down a narrow lane. She really liked being in charge.

"But we didn't come this way before," said Otto.

"So what?" shrugged Scarlett. "The sign's pointing this way. Come on!"

They followed the narrow lane for quite a while as it weaved this way and that. It finally led to a big hill. They climbed it and, when they reached the top, the children got quite a surprise.

"Hey, look!" said Otto. At the foot of the hill was the Highland Games camp. They could also

see Aunt Beastly's small stone cottage on the opposite side of the loch. They had walked round it in a great big loop and now they were stuck across the water.

"Look how far away the cottage is!" said Martha. "It'll take us forever to walk all the way back."

"Don't worry," said Otto. "We can row over there."

"But what if we fall in the water?" Martha whispered.

"We won't," said Scarlett. "Come on!"

They walked down the hill, the Highland Games camp in view. On the top of the large marquee was a big red tartan flag. It fluttered in the breeze coming off the water.

Otto was tempted to stay and watch the competitors train. But he still had the scrapbook.

They needed to get back and figure out a new plan.

The children skirted round the edge of the Games field. Near the loch, they saw an old stone barn.

Its ivy-covered walls were crumbling and some tiles had come off its roof. Its heavy wooden door was painted green, though most of the paint had peeled off, and its windows were long, thin slits.

Near the barn was a bank leading down to the loch. And there, tied up on the edge of the water, Otto saw several rowing boats.

Carefully the children climbed into one – first Scarlett, then Otto and finally Martha, who was trembling worse than ever.

Otto took the oars and started to row back, while a shaky Martha gripped the boat's side.

Suddenly, when they were halfway across the loch, Martha gave an ear-splitting shriek. "Arrgh! Otto! Scarlett! *Look* – down there!"

She pointed a finger at the surface of the water, where giant bubbles were exploding all around. Great rumbling creaks and groans were coming from deep under the water.

Otto stopped rowing. There was something down there, under their boat! Something that made lots of bubbles. Uh-oh...

Otto felt his heart start to race. No ordinary fish would blow bubbles like this!

"Sh-shark!" spluttered Martha, her face ghostly white.

"No!" beamed Scarlett. "It's a sea monster! I've heard there are monsters up here in the lochs! Oh, bother – if only I'd brought *Fred*, I could have tried to catch it."

"What!" squeaked Martha. "Scarlett, are you crazy? Otto, what do we do?"

Otto shook his head. "I dunno." The detective side of him was filled with excitement. But the other side – the skinny nine-year-old bit – seemed to be telling him they ought to scarper... "Hold tight!" he cried, and started to row faster than he'd ever rowed before. He didn't look back, he just rowed and rowed and rowed!

As soon as they reached the other side of the loch they belted up the bank, their thoughts full of monsters, and burst into the cottage.

"Phew!" panted Otto. They'd made it!

Aunt Beastly had only just got back, too. "Why are you so hot and bothered?" she snapped. She seemed in a worse mood than ever.

"Um," said Otto. "W-we were just playing!"

"What?" barked Aunt Beastly. "Playing, you say? Well, you are clearly not playing the right sort of games at all!"

Martha quickly changed the subject. "Did any neighbours say they'd help you build pens?"

"Pah!" spat Aunt Beastly. "Waste of time! Mary McNab's over at the Games and Hamish wasn't on his boat. Then I tried Angus who runs the village pub, but—"

"He's my dad!" Donald cut in.

"But *he* wasn't there either," Aunt Beastly snapped. "Only Mora and Barry can help. They're coming after lunch, so they say."

She then asked the children how they had got on finding helpers from the village.

"Um, most people weren't in either," said Otto, his fingers crossed behind his back.

"Anyway!" beamed Donald. "I've got some news!"

"What?" Aunt Beastly asked suspiciously. She narrowed her piggy eyes.

"Well," said Donald, "some men called round when you were all out. They wanted to buy a baby boar!"

"I certainly hope you didn't sell them one!" Aunt Beastly said with a scowl.

"I didn't!" smiled Donald, looking mighty smug.

Otto and his sisters exchanged worried looks.

"How many men?" Otto whispered to Donald when Aunt Beastly had gone to make lunch.

Donald counted on his fingers. "Three!" he said. "A fat one, a tall one and one with a dear old granny!"

The children didn't utter a word but they were all thinking exactly the same thing. The Unstoppables had found the cottage. The baddies were on to them.

B ack at the campsite, the Unstoppables were huddled in their tent.

"A complete waste of time, going to that boar farm," growled Stinkerton. "All that trouble and the scrapbook wasn't even there!"

He ran a hand through his hair. It was greasy! Like *Lenny's*. What was happening to him? He was losing the plot. And his fingers were trembling. *Trembling!*

All because of those three dratted kids. They had turned him into a quivering wreck! "This is all your fault!" he shouted at Lenny.

"W-what?" Lenny spluttered. "How come? It was *you* who—"

"Don't you *dare* blame me!" roared Stinkerton.

Stinkerton's eyes were narrowed in rage and a vein was throbbing in his temple. His fists were clenched, his teeth gritted and his bottlebrush moustache – usually neatly styled – was sticking out in clumps. He looked like a madman.

"Don't you ever, EVER blame me!" roared Stinkerton. "Nothing in my entire life has *ever* been my fault. It all started with that museum job. *You* should have memorized the layout better."

"But," squeaked Lenny, "what about him?" He pointed a finger at Doug. "If anyone's to blame, it's that pudding!" he cried. "Him and his stupid cheese and onion crisps giving our disguise away! It wasn't me who got careless – it was *him*."

"Well, I don't think it's *my* fault," Doug muttered. "Just because I'm fond of crisps. Everyone needs a hobby, don't they?"

"SHUT UP!" Stinkerton leaped up and tried pacing about but the tent was infuriatingly pokey. "I can't think straight in this mouldy piece of rag!" he thundered.

He closed his eyes and took a deep, calming breath. He needed to get a grip. Right now. Otherwise he'd never get the scrapbook back from those kids.

"Right," said Stinkerton, sitting back down and smoothing out his itchy kilt. "We won't get anywhere arguing like this. Let's start with what we know. The scrapbook wasn't anywhere in the house so that means the kids are keeping it close. They must be taking it with them wherever they go."

"O-or it could have been eaten by a boar?" suggested Doug. "We could examine their poo to see if—"

"No!" bellowed Stinkerton. "Forget the poo, okay!" He thought for a moment, then spoke again. "If that dim-witted lad has told them he had visitors, our cover could be blown."

"But they won't know it was us," said Lenny. "It was just three blokes looking for a boar for their granny."

"But the kids will *guess* it was us!" cried Stinkerton, his temper rising again. As much as it pained him to admit it, those kids were clever. "After what happened on the train," he went on, "they'll have guessed we're on to them. So we'll have to tail *them* to get the book back. And don't you dare argue. I am right!"

"Or, how about," Doug blundered on, "we break into the cottage and steal the scrapbook back tonight."

"No – the house is too muddly!" scowled Stinkerton. "All those squealing little beasts. There are too many things that could go wrong.

It would be better to find the kids tomorrow at the Games and snatch the scrapbook off them there. I'm pretty certain they'll come and they're bound to bring it with them. We'll get it then."

While the Unstoppables plotted, the children were sitting in their tent in the garden, working out what *their* next move should be.

Otto placed the scrapbook on the floor, staring at it through his long, scruffy fringe. "What would Montague Plum do?" he said, thinking hard.

There was silence as Otto went through Plum's cases. One of them might just help. He thought of *The Case of the Eiffel Star Gem*. In that episode, the robbers – a gang of notorious cat burglars – were after the world-famous Eiffel

Star Gem, a priceless diamond kept in a secret underground vault beneath the Eiffel Tower in Paris.

Plum finally set the robbers up and captured them by sending them on a wild goose chase. He led them to believe that the diamond was being moved from its underground vault. Naturally, the robbers tried to track where it was going. But the real diamond wasn't moved at all – Plum used a *fake* one that looked identical.

The robbers followed the fake diamond to a ruined monastery high in the French Alps where Plum was waiting for them. He trapped the robbers, then had them carted off to jail.

Maybe, thought Otto, he and his sisters could do something similar with the scrapbook?

Suddenly Otto leaped to his feet. "That's it!" he cried. "That's how we get them!"

"What?" Martha looked up at him. "Have you thought of a plan?"

"Yes!" cried Otto. "A brilliant one!"

"Don't tell me," tutted Scarlett. "It's a Plum one, right?"

"So what?" said Otto. "He's an ace detective. Anyway, it's not exactly the same – we've got to change bits to suit our case."

"Go on then," sighed Scarlett. "We might as well hear it, I suppose."

"Okay," said Otto, "my plan's a bit similar to *The Case of the Eiffel Star Gem*. We make a *fake* scrapbook for the robbers to go after and eventually we let them steal it. In this fake book there'll be a ransom note telling the robbers where to come if they want their *real* book back. They'll be so cross that they've been tricked that they won't be thinking straight any more and they'll come to wherever we tell them. Then we'll be waiting there to capture them. Ha!"

"But, Otto," said Martha, "that sounds really dangerous." Her fingers moved to Pod's cord.

"Don't pull the cord, Martha!" cried Otto. "You were brave last week. It'll be okay!"

"And what about the *real* scrapbook?" Martha trembled. "What do we do with that? They might come round here anytime to steal it – even tonight." She gulped.

"I know," said Otto. "We hide it somewhere else. And we do it before bedtime."

"Okay," said Scarlett. "But I've found another problem. You said you'll let them steal the *fake* scrapbook, right?"

"Yeah," said Otto. "So?"

"So surely they'll *see* that it's not the real one the minute they steal it," Scarlett said.

"Then they'll t-turn on us," Martha stuttered. "We'll be done for!"

"Unless," said Scarlett, her mind racing ahead, "the robbers don't *see* it's a fake book until they're back in their hideout. Maybe it could be in Otto's rucksack when they steal it."

"So they'll steal Otto's bag with the book inside?" asked Martha.

"Exactly!" Otto chipped in, trying to sound really cool. "That's what I'd planned all along."

His cheeks had turned pink. He was a very bad liar.

"Yeah!" giggled Scarlett. "Right!"

The children talked their plan through a bit more. Stinkerton's scrapbook had a shiny silver cover, so they'd have to wrap an old book of their aunt's in tinfoil to make the fake one look the same. They'd also need to copy out the title in identical handwriting.

"Otto," said Martha, still looking worried. "Where can we hide the real scrapbook? And is that the place we're going to lure the robbers to, so that we can capture them?"

"Yeah," said Otto, chewing the end of his pencil like Montague Plum always did. "I was thinking it should be somewhere gloomy and dark, so we can hide in the shadows – like an old monastery, maybe?"

Scarlett sniggered. "How many monasteries have you seen round here?"

There was silence.

"Yeah. None," said Scarlett. "Probably the closest thing is that old barn we came across earlier. Remember – the one near the Games field? It looked like no one ever goes in there because it's falling apart."

"Exactly!" said Otto, blushing again. "I was just thinking that, too – cos..." He stopped and racked his brains, trying to think up a better reason than Scarlett's.

"Oh, yeah... Because that barn is right by the Games field. So when we've got the robbers trapped we'll be able to nip out and get some competitors to help us cart them off to jail. And before you say anything," Otto went on, "I know the police in Muldoon are useless, so we'll take

the robbers somewhere else."

He whipped out a tourist map he'd picked up at the Muldoon police station earlier. "Dunroaming's not far away," he said. "It looks like a much bigger place than Muldoon, so I bet it'll have a better police station. We'll take the robbers there. Job done!"

The children knew they needed to act fast now to keep one step ahead of the Unstoppables. The Games were starting tomorrow afternoon and they had a lot to do before then.

"We should plant the scrapbook in the barn tonight," Otto said.

"Hold on!" shrieked Martha. "That barn's across the loch. If we row over in the dark, that monster-thing will get us!"

Otto thought for a moment. "Well, we could walk the long way round, through town."

"But that's no fun," groaned Scarlett. "I want to catch that monster and train it up as a pet!"

"Nope, we're walking," Otto said. "However tough you think you are, Scarlett, you'll never be able to tame a monster!"

"Spoilsport," Scarlett glowered.

But before getting started on making the fake scrapbook, the children had to get out of Aunt Beastly's pen-making party.

Otto sent Squawk off to scope out what Aunt Beastly was doing. He checked the screen on his tracker watch and saw that she was in the kitchen with two strange people, who he guessed to be Mora and Barry Stewart.

"Aunt Beastly located," Otto said. "The neighbours are with her. This calls for a super-fast disappearing act!"

Zac, Otto's tent, had two zips on the door.

The first zip was just an ordinary one but the second zip (thanks to Henrig) made the tent blend into its surroundings. In other words, Otto's tent would become perfectly camouflaged.

Zip! With a faint *pop!* the olive green tent began to change. It was like someone was painting over it with an invisible paintbrush!

In just a few seconds, Zac would disappear from sight, leaving only a clump of purple heather in its place.

"Bye bye, Aunt Beastly!" sniggered Otto.

Henrig had designed Zac for bird-watching, but there was no reason why the tent couldn't be used for vanishing from the prying eyes of Aunt Beastly. So, even though Zac (and everyone inside) would actually still be there, to Aunt Beastly's eyes it would be invisible.

The children heard their aunt stomp outside and they froze at once. Although the tent might *look* like heather now, the transformation didn't block out sound, so if they were noisy, Aunt Beastly would still hear them.

"Otto! Martha! Scarlett!" she boomed.

They sat, as quiet as church mice.

"Och, what a pity!" said a woman, who Otto guessed to be Mora. "It doesn't look like the wee kiddies are about."

"Perhaps they're off playing," a man replied. This had to be Barry, Mora's husband. "Och well – you've got us to build the pens, eh, Bessie. We'll do it!"

The children heard their aunt snort. "That's hardly the point! Children! Where *are* you?" she yelled.

Aunt Beastly took another step towards the heather bush, bent down and peered around. "The tent was here. Just here!"

She was almost touching the invisible walls. The children spied her eye and one hairy nostril through a small gap in the tent door.

"Oooohhh!" she puffed and a blast of pongy breath wafted in. It smelled like boars – little baldy-tailed boars.

Suddenly Scarlett got a dreadful urge to giggle. She snorted and Martha clapped a hand over her mouth.

"Shhh!" Otto mouthed, his eyes wide.

A moment later, their aunt straightened up and her hairy face disappeared.

"Well, really!" she boomed, gazing through the trees and up to the hill behind the house. "The *one* time I need help, the children slope off to play camping up in the fields! Just wait till they reappear tonight. Just wait!"

The children heard them move off down the garden and Otto peeped out of the tent door.

"They've gone into the shed," he whispered to his sisters. "Probably to get some tools. If we

134

need stuff for making the fake scrapbook, we'd better get it now."

Scarlett and Martha crept out of the tent and tiptoed through the open cottage door. Scarlett went to find an old book of Aunt Beastly's while Martha got some tinfoil from the kitchen drawer.

Meanwhile, Otto stayed in the tent and rifled through his rucksack for some pens and paper to write the ransom note on.

His sisters were back before he knew it.

"Aunt Beastly's still in the shed," whispered Martha. "I heard them as we came back."

"Okay," Otto nodded. "Got what we need?"

"Of course!" said Scarlett, grinning.

The book Scarlett had chosen was called *Becoming Best Buddies with Boars.* While she was covering it, Martha practised copying Stinkerton's handwriting, to make the title look just the same as on the real scrapbook.

Otto, meanwhile, wrote the letter to go inside...

Dear Sebastian Stinkerton,

If you want your real scrapbook back, come to the old barn by the loch at sunset. If you don't, we'll tell the police on you. Oh, and bring money (a lot).

Yours Sincerely,
Otto, Martha and Scarlett Crumb

Now they just had to wait until dark. Then the plan to hide the *real* scrapbook could begin...

Chapter EIGHT

That night, after a telling-off from Aunt Beastly for disappearing earlier, the children stood outside, flying Martha's Sky Dancers through the inky sky.

The Sky Dancers looked like real fireflies, with shimmering papery wings and bottoms alight with bright sparkles.

As the children watched them, they talked about the Loch Greythorn monster.

"I think," said Scarlett, "it's a vampire jellyfish with great sharp fangs and claw-covered tentacles and snotty stuff pouring from its nose."

"Nah, jellyfish don't have noses," said Otto. "It's probably a cross between a giant spider and a crab, with a bit of werewolf thrown in!" He whipped out his notebook and did a quick sketch. "Massive pincers all over the place, eight legs, a hairy head, a big mouth with huge teeth and three billion eyes that turn you to stone with one single stare."

Martha gulped and snapped Otto's notebook shut. "That's enough!" she cried. They might not be crossing the loch later, but even the *thought* of the monster terrified her.

At that moment, Aunt Beastly thumped outside carrying a tray of mugs. Curls of white steam were rising from them.

"Mmmm – hot chocolate!" Scarlett beamed. "My favourite!"

"No," said Aunt Beastly, passing them the drinks. "This is much tastier – hot cabbage water!"

The children's mouths dropped open.

"Now, I'm off to bed!" Their aunt smiled. "Are you absolutely sure you don't want to sleep in the cottage tonight?"

All the boars were finally in their new pens – except for Basil, who always slept at the foot of Aunt Beastly's bed.

"W-we like it in the tent," Otto said. "It's more of an adventure out here!" He glanced at his sisters, who quickly nodded. It would be easier to creep off and hide Stinkerton's scrapbook if they stayed outside for one more night.

Aunt Beastly shrugged. "Well, don't be late to bed! The Games start tomorrow and you don't want to be tired."

"Do they go on late, Aunt Bessie?" asked Otto.

"Really late!" she boomed. "The last event tomorrow happens at dusk – a rowing race across the loch."

The children glanced at each other, thinking about the monster.

"And *then* there's an opening-day firework display," their aunt chuntered on. "You don't want to be tired for *that* now, do you?" With that, she marched inside for her "beauty sleep".

The children waited another half-hour to make sure Aunt Beastly was asleep, then they put away the Sky Dancers, packed the real scrapbook into Otto's rucksack and turned on their torches.

"Right then," whispered Otto. "Let's go!"

They tiptoed towards the hill behind the cottage. It was going to be a long walk. Scarlett led the way through a clump of Scots Pines but as they walked under the thick canopy of branches – *snap!*

"What was that?" gasped Martha.

"Don't panic!" Otto said quietly. "It's probably just a fox."

The children took another step forward then... *Snap!* There it was again.

"The Unstoppables!" hissed Otto. "Quick!" He nudged his sisters and they turned and crept back out of the trees. Otto was so spooked he could hardly breathe. "Right! Get into the boat!"

"No!" squeaked Martha.

"Yes! It's the only way!" Otto jumped into the rowing boat and his sisters followed.

A suffocating mist rose off the water in low, sweeping curls. To Martha it looked like long white fingers beckoning them to a certain watery doom. "What if the monster gets us?" she gulped, as Otto grabbed hold of the oars.

"We don't even know there *is* a monster yet," replied Otto.

"Spoilsport," muttered Scarlett.

Otto started to row as fast as he could. His sisters glanced back to their aunt's garden but they couldn't see anything there...

"That snapping noise," Martha breathed. "It might have just been an escaped boar."

"Who knows?" said Otto. "But I didn't fancy hanging round to find out!"

He carried on rowing until the old stone barn came into view through the mist. It was lit by a pale, silvery moon. The Games field was deserted now, as all the competitors were back in their tents for the night.

"Nearly there," Otto whispered. "And no sign of any monsters."

"Yet," Martha added in a hushed voice.

The children rowed past the old fishing tug where Hamish McTavy lived. It was dark in there, too, and Otto imagined a grumpy old fisherman tucked up in bed, snoring.

When they reached the other side of the loch, they climbed out of the boat, sighing with relief. They tied the boat to a mooring ring and crept up the bank towards the barn.

"It looks kind of h-haunted," Martha shivered.

"Yeah, it does," grinned Scarlett. "I've always wanted to meet a real live ghost!"

Otto shone his torch at the barn. It looked a lot spookier than when they'd passed it earlier. Ivy wriggled up its crumbling walls like a tangle of green snakes and its slit-like windows seemed to be glowing, like the barn was watching them.

"Are there lights on in there?" Martha murmured.

"It's just the moon's reflection," Otto said. "Don't worry."

Suddenly an owl hooted and they jumped.

"I'm really not sure about this," sniffed Martha.

Otto edged his sister towards the barn door. "Ready?" he whispered.

"Ready," they both replied.

Otto placed his hand on the door and was about to push it open when he noticed that it was already ajar. Then from inside the barn they heard a man's voice – and it sounded very grumpy...

"The monster's a right scary beast. *Look*. See the red anger in her eyes!"

"That might be!" came another voice. It was an old woman this time and she sounded even crabbier than the man. "But what good is it if she can't finish the job?"

"Aye," came a muffled chorus of groans.

The children gaped. There were lots of people in there. And it sounded like they'd captured the monster from the loch!

Otto was puzzled. If the monster *was* in the barn, why hadn't it ripped everyone limb from limb? And why wasn't it making any sound? He'd expect a scary monster to be roaring and gnashing its teeth...

"I want to go," Martha whispered.

"I want to see the monster!" said Scarlett.

Otto moved closer to the door as the woman's

voice sounded again...

"Hamish McTavy, look at the beast. She's just not right and you know it!"

"She *will* be!" roared Hamish. "Just give me a chance!"

"But she has to do her worst *tomorrow*, man!" the old woman shouted back. "You've run out of time."

"No!" barked Hamish. "Rattlebones will be ready!"

The children didn't understand. The monster wasn't "right" ... they were putting it back tomorrow, so that she could "do her worst"... What did it all mean?

Then Otto's eyes widened. "The Games!" he gasped. "Aunt Beastly said that tomorrow night there'll be people *racing* across the loch. They're sending the monster to eat them up!"

With that, Martha let out a squeak of terror. Before they could stop her, she pulled Pod's cord. The life jacket inflated into a bubble around her and she rolled off down the bank.

"*Martha!*" Otto yelped. "Come back!"

Scarlett raced after her but as Otto went to follow, the barn door suddenly burst open and a wrinkled hand grabbed him by the ear.

"Arrrrrgh! Let go! Let go!" Otto cried as an old man pulled him into the barn.

As soon as Martha heard the cry she tugged the cord and Pod deflated. Scarlett helped Martha to her feet again and the girls raced to the barn.

"Oi!" yelled Scarlett. "Let my brother go!"

They dashed into the barn and immediately heard the door slam shut behind them.

The children gasped as it dawned on them. They were trapped.

Chapter NINE

The gloomy barn was lit by torches. The old man had one and, further off, the children could make out shadowy figures all holding torches, too.

Scarlett flew at the old man, who was still gripping Otto's ear, and started to pinch like mad.

"Get off!" roared the man. "You nasty little crab!"

"Oh, please!" wailed Martha. "Please let my brother go!"

Then one of the shadowy figures called, "Hamish, look! They're just kids!"

Mora Stewart hurried forward with her husband, Barry, at her side. The children recognized them from earlier that day when Squawk had beamed back pictures of them chatting to Aunt Beastly at the cottage.

As more people scurried out of the shadows,

Hamish peered down at the children and they saw his face properly for the first time.

Hamish McTavy had ruddy red cheeks and his nose was big and purple. He wore a yellow sou'wester and dark green wellies, and he looked very weary indeed.

"What do you think you're doing?" asked Hamish.

A scary old woman shuffled up. "Them kids have been spying on us!" she spat.

"We're not spies," said Otto. "We thought the barn was empty."

"Our aunt lives over the loch," gulped Martha. "Bessie Crumb."

Hamish let go of Otto's ear.

"Let me see them!" said a giant of a man, striding towards them. "My Donald works at your aunt's place, you know! I'm Angus McDonald. Who are you? And what are you doing wandering round here at night?"

To brush over the second question, Otto started with his name instead...

"I'm Otto."

"I'm Martha."

"I'm ... *mind your own business!*"

"She's Scarlett," said Otto quickly.

Angus McDonald burst into a chuckle. He was a chubby-cheeked man with a shiny bald head and a bushy snow-white beard.

"So, what of our chat did you hear?" he asked with a friendly smile. "When you *weren't* spying right outside, I mean? Didn't hear nothing about the monster, did you?"

"Don't tell them there's a *monster*, you goose!" Hamish roared. "They might not have heard us saying that."

"We did," said Scarlett, her nose in the air. "So there!"

Otto glanced around curiously. Where *was* this monster anyway?

"So you know about the monster?" Hamish growled.

"Well ... yeah, I suppose." Otto nodded.

"And that's not all!" Scarlett sniffed. "We know you're setting your monster on people at the Games tomorrow, too!"

Hamish frowned. "What's she on about? The monster's not gonna get a soul."

"Is, too!" cried Scarlett. "We heard you, so there!"

With that Martha took a tiny step forward, summoning up the nerve to speak. "We heard, um ... *her* s-say–" she pointed at the old lady– "that tomorrow the monster had to 'do her worst'. That means *eat* people, d-doesn't it?"

"No!" cried Hamish. "Rattlebones could never do that!"

Hamish and Angus exchanged glances. Then Hamish strode over to a thick black curtain. "Otto, Martha, Mind Your Own Business – meet Rattlebones!"

He drew back the curtain.

The children gasped and huddled together, their hearts pounding. Martha grabbed Otto's

arm. Then they stopped and looked more closely.

"H-hang on a minute," Martha stuttered.

"It's not ... not ... *real*?" said Otto.

"Poo," groaned Scarlett. "What is it then?"

The Loch Greythorn Monster – or Rattlebones, as she had been named – was, in fact, a mighty big junk model. And, as junk models go, she was ace!

"It was *her*!" cried Otto. "Those bubbles in the loch when we crossed it this afternoon!"

"Oh," tutted Scarlett. "I'll never catch a real monster now!"

Rattlebones might not be real, thought Otto, *but she does look fierce.* She looked like a cross between a giant cockroach and an ugly giraffe.

"Me and Angus built her," said Hamish, in answer to the astonished looks on the children's faces.

The monster's body was made from an upturned fishing boat. Instead of legs, she had duck-like feet that dangled down.

These feet, Otto saw, were flippers, hanging down from a thick length of rope that coiled around her whole body. The end of the rope was then attached to a propeller-like tail.

Her long, thin neck had been made from strong chicken wire filled with jagged rocks.

These rocks made the monster look ever so scaly and menacing.

Her head was a sturdy beer barrel. Two holes had been cut out of it and bright fishing buoys wedged inside them. These made the beast look like it had flaming red eyes.

Finally, all along her neck and domed back ran a trail of spikes made from canvas sails edged with wire.

Otto was really impressed, especially when he spied a small door on the side of the monster's body, housing a motor to bring her to life.

"But what does the monster actually *do*?" he said.

"Ah," sighed Hamish, "it's what she *doesn't* do that's the problem!"

"What do you mean?" Otto asked. "Why have you built a sea monster? Just for fun?"

"Fun," tutted Hamish, glowering. "There's no time for fun round here any more. We've built her to save Muldoon from witherin' away!"

"You see, the thing is," Hamish went on, "tomorrow a load of TV folk will be up for the Highland Games. And while they're here, we need to show the world a wee glimpse of old Rattlebones."

Rattlebones, he then told them, was meant to

stay hidden under the loch until the TV crews were filming the fireworks on the first night of the Games. Then she was supposed to burst out of the water just long enough for the world to think that a sea monster lived in Loch Greythorn – just like the one in Loch Ness!

Hamish nodded. "Once folk have had a peep of our monster, they're gonna want to see more! So they'll flock here. Flock to our beautiful Muldoon, all year round. And *that'll* mean they'll need places to stay and things to eat, and so on. So all our guest houses and Angus's pub will be full to bursting. Then people here will *work* again and the old place will be saved!"

"Mary used to have a tearoom in the good old days," said Angus, "but now it's boarded up. And Hamish ran fishing trips on the loch, too."

"Aye," sighed Hamish, remembering. "So the

monster's our only hope, see? Except–" he shook his head– "she just won't rise."

"What do you mean, she won't rise?" asked Otto.

"Exactly that," Hamish replied. "We've tried and tried but Rattlebones simply will not rise out of the water! She'll sink down under the loch, all right. But we cannee get her to pop back up."

"So she'll niver get caught on TV tomorrow!" snapped the old woman.

Now Hamish was slowly nodding his head. "Aye, you might be right, Mary. Maybe it is too late and I've failed."

And suddenly everyone fell silent.

After a while, Hamish looked at the children. "Well, a broken sea monster ain't your problem. And 'tis time you were getting back home."

Martha, Otto and Scarlett nodded and

made their way to the door. Then suddenly Otto remembered the scrapbook. With all the commotion, he hadn't managed to hide it away.

He quickly slipped it out of his rucksack, slid it under a bale of hay, then followed his sisters outside.

"Bye then," called Hamish, waving. "And remember – not a word about Rattlebones."

"We promise," Otto called back through the darkness. "But don't give up, Mr McTavy. I'm sure you'll get your monster rising somehow."

As they rowed back across the loch, Otto felt sorry for the villagers. He wondered if *he* could help make the monster rise. He helped his dad out with his inventions all the time...

"So where can we hide the scrapbook now?" asked Scarlett.

"Already done it!" smiled Otto. He told his sisters exactly where it was. Now everything was set for tomorrow.

When they got back to their tent, Otto's brain was still buzzing. As his sisters slept, he was burrowed down inside his sleeping bag. His torch was propped up as he scribbled down ideas of how he might get Rattlebones to rise. He had a hunch. And *if* he was right, the solution might be simpler than everyone thought...

Chapter

TEN

The next morning Otto woke before dawn. Today was a very big day – the Games were starting and he and his sisters were ready to put the next step of their plan into action. He'd also thought of an idea last night to get Rattlebones rising out of the loch. Now he just had to go and tell Hamish. But first he wanted to note down the plan for how they were going to stop the Unstoppables once and for all!

Otto took out his notebook and began to write...

Step 1: Otto, Martha and Scarlett (Code: O, M + S) go to the Highland Games.

Step 2: Stinkerton spots O's rucksack and thinks that his scrapbook is inside.

Step 3: The robbers go after the bag. O, M + S run away to make it believable but eventually let them steal it.

Step 4: Back at their hideout, the Unstoppables discover that the book is fake. (Shock! Horror!) They find the note telling them to come to the old barn at sunset if they want the real book back.

Step 5: O, M + S wait in the barn. S to hang upside down from a rafter with Fred, ready to trap the Unstoppables.

Step 6: The robbers arrive and S traps them in Fred's net. M runs out to get help while O + S guard the robbers.

Step 7: Competitors help O, M + S cart the Unstoppables off to Dunroaming police station. They go to jail for a long time...

Step 8: Either a) O, M + S are awarded medals. Or b) Aunt Beastly is cross and makes O, M + S shovel up boar poop — possibly forever!

Otto got dressed and crept out of the tent. It was only just light. He got into the boat and rowed across the loch, certain that Hamish would still be in the barn, trying to sort the problem.

When Otto got there he discovered he was right. A glum-looking Hamish was sitting in the barn, Rattlebones at his side, wet and still.

"Worked all night, I have," sighed Hamish. "But Mary's right, it's no good. Rattlebones won't rise up out of the water and that's that."

Otto pulled up an old barrel and sat down next to Hamish.

"That's why I'm here, Mr McTavy," he said. "I think it might be an air lock."

"What was that, laddie?" Hamish yawned.

"Why Rattlebones won't go up," replied Otto. "I think it's an air lock in the ballast tank pump."

To Otto this made perfect sense. They could let water *in* to make Rattlebones sink but they couldn't pump it back *out* again (which would make her rise) *if* there was an air lock in the pump.

Hamish looked up and rubbed his eyes.

"My dad's an inventor," Otto went on, "and I help him out all the time. He made me this toy submarine once that had just the same problem. It stopped working – it wouldn't float back up to the top of the pond. We checked everything and then Dad looked at the pump. There was an air lock. I think Rattlebones has got the same problem!"

Otto helped Hamish investigate the pump. They opened a control valve to release any air lock, then they closed it and checked the motor one more time. Hamish manoeuvred the monster on to her loading trolley and wheeled her out to the loch. Otto kept watch to make sure no one was about as Hamish carefully lowered her into the water so she sank right down.

"Right, let's see if she'll rise," said Hamish.

Otto crossed his fingers. They would have to be quick before people on the campsite got up for the day and started milling around.

Hamish thrust a hand into his pocket and pulled out a remote control. He switched it on and it gave a low bleep.

Otto watched as Hamish flicked a lever on the front of the remote to *UP.*

Nothing happened.

Then suddenly...

Whoosh!

Rattlebones's head burst up out of the loch, sending fountains of water everywhere. Her red eyes were on fire and her rocky neck rattled like thunder.

"You did it!" cried Otto, as Hamish sent the monster back down under the water.

"No – *you* did it!" Hamish smiled. "Thank you, laddie! Thank you!"

When Otto got back to the tent he woke his sisters and told them about Rattlebones.

"Well done!" beamed Martha.

Even Scarlett thought it was "quite cool".

"Thanks," said Otto. "But now for the Unstoppables."

He whipped out his notebook and took the others through the plan step-by-step.

That done, they went into the cottage, where Aunt Beastly was busy writing something.

"Now, the Games aren't starting until *two*," she boomed, "so first I need help with the boars. And no sloping off like yesterday!"

She rattled off a list of jobs...

"Martha! Poop control and tail inspection."

"Poop control?" Martha gasped. "But, um ... what's that?"

"Why, scooping up poop!" Aunt Beastly nodded. "With a shovel!"

"But poop is full of germs!" Martha shuddered.

Aunt Beastly pretended not to hear. "And tail inspection means checking for any sign of tuftiness!"

She turned to Otto. "Otto!" she barked.

"Poop control and bubble baths!"

"But boars *hate* baths," Otto groaned. "They'll trump in the water. Yuck!"

"And make sure you clean behind their dear little ears!" Aunt Beastly added.

Finally she looked at Scarlett.

"I am NOT doing poop," Scarlett announced.

"Stuff and nonsense!" said Aunt Beastly. "We *all* do poop!"

"NO WAY!" cried Scarlett.

With a grunt, Aunt Beastly bustled outside and the children trooped glumly behind.

"I hate boars!" Scarlett said in her stroppiest voice.

The morning passed in a whirl of whiffy boar poop. None of the boars' bald, skinny tails looked like they'd *ever* tuft and Basil trumped in his bubble bath the whole time!

By one o'clock the children stank and were quite worn out. For lunch Aunt Beastly served one of her favourites – sludgy cabbage soup. Then they got ready to row across to the Games.

Scarlett was already wearing her Creeper-Sneakers and holding Fred, ready for putting their plan into action later.

"You won't need a fishing rod, dear," said Aunt Beastly. "There's no fishing allowed while the Games are on."

"But I *want* to take it," said Scarlett.

Aunt Beastly sniffed.

"Don't be silly. You'll have to lug it around all day!"

"I don't care!" said Scarlett haughtily. "You lug Basil around all day!" She glared at Basil, tucked under her aunt's arm.

"That's totally different!" Aunt Beastly bristled. She gazed down at the hairy little creature and a dreamy look filled her eyes. "Basie-Boo is Mummy's ickle baby!" she cooed. Then she strode to the door. "Off we go!"

When they arrived at the Highland Games, it was packed with people all hurrying along to watch the opening ceremony. Lots of them were waving little tartan flags and the children had blow-up cabers.

"Come on then, children!" Aunt Beastly said.

"Follow me!"

They joined the crowd lining the big parade field to watch the marching bands. Hundreds of bagpipers were puffing out screechy tunes while processing around the field in neat formations.

Basil seemed to like the music. He was definitely jigging about in Aunt Beastly's arms.

"Look at his little tusks!" she beamed. "He's smiling!"

The children, however, were thinking about the Unstoppables.

"Maybe Squawk can spot the robbers," Otto whispered to his sisters. He pressed a button on his watch and Squawk fluttered into the air.

The problem was, Otto hadn't a clue how the robbers would be disguised. He just knew he was looking for a short, fat one, one who was tall and thin, and sly, smart Stinkerton, with the

neat bottlebrush moustache.

Otto scanned the screen on his wristband while Squawk flapped above the crowds. But there were *hundreds* of people, of all shapes and sizes. It was no good. It was like finding a needle in a haystack!

Finally Otto pressed the "call Squawk" button and, a few moments later, the little metal spy-bird came to land on his shoulder.

"Any luck?" Martha whispered.

Otto shook his head. "It's too busy," he sighed. "Can you keep Squawk safe in your bag until later?"

"Okay," Martha replied, popping Squawk away.

After the bands, the contests began and the children managed to persuade Aunt Beastly to let them go off on their own.

The sun had peeped out from behind a cloud and the air buzzed with excitement as they wandered round the Games searching out the robbers.

They stopped by the caber-tossing field, where huge tree trunks were flying about. A big crowd of spectators were watching, but the Unstoppables didn't seem to be among them.

Next they passed the hammer-throwers, who were slinging metal balls through the air.

"No robbers here either," said Martha with a sigh. "Where *are* they?"

The children did a circuit of the entire place but the Unstoppables were nowhere to be seen.

"They've got to be here somewhere," said Otto. "They've *got* to!"

From the very moment the Games had opened, the Unstoppables had been searching for the children, too. Every time Stinkerton thought he'd spotted them, it turned out to be other children. The place was packed with them!

Eventually, the robbers tried the food tent.

"The kids will need to eat at some point," said Stinkerton. "Follow me!"

"Shhh," hissed Otto, as he passed the food tent.

All three children froze. Martha and Scarlett had heard it, too – a great rumbling burp.

One of the Unstoppables had burped *just* like that outside their house in Sharkstooth Bay last week.

Otto peeped inside the tent. There was a group of burly caber-tossers and a couple of women drinking milkshakes. Then he saw three Highland dancers. Two of them were sipping tea and the third was eating...

"Cheese and onion crisps!" Otto whispered. He knew the fat robber was fond of those. He nudged his sisters. "Look, that's them!"

Martha started to tremble. "A-are you sure?"

Otto nodded. One was short and fat, the other tall and thin, and the third looked sly and smarmy.

Otto unzipped his rucksack just enough for a corner of the fake scrapbook to poke out. He was sure Stinkerton wouldn't be able to resist.

The children marched in and went straight past the baddies. As they did, Otto said loudly, "Let me know if you see any *robbers* about!"

Martha gulped, resisting the urge to tug Pod's cord. "We c-can't let them steal the *scrapbook* out of your *rucksack*!"

At the counter, Otto ordered three oatcakes and snuck a glimpse at the Unstoppables. They'd spotted him and his sisters all right. Now he just had to wait for the robbers to make their move on the rucksack. Then the chase would begin, just as they had planned.

As Mary McNab turned around to get some plates, Otto felt his rucksack being tugged. He gripped the straps and held on tightly. "Oi! No, you don't!" he cried, making his voice sound surprised.

Stinkerton tugged at the bag again, as Lenny and Doug closed in.

"Let go!" shouted Otto. He couldn't let Stinkerton grab it yet, or it would look too easy. He had to make the whole thing look real, so he turned to his sisters. "RUN!"

Scarlett snatched up a rock cake and hurled it at Stinkerton's nose.

Instinctively Stinkerton let go of the bag to shield his face from the missile. "No!" he roared, as the children raced out. "STOP!"

As he ran, Otto glanced back to check that the robbers were after them. They dodged through the crowds, pretending to hurry but making sure the robbers could keep up. Soon Otto could let Stinkerton capture the rucksack.

"Eeek!" squeaked the children, swerving round a policeman brandishing a baguette.

"Friend or foe?" muttered Constable Batty, as the robbers pushed him out of the way.

"What do you think?" yelled Stinkerton, racing past. "Idiot!"

But then, as the children passed the dancing stage, the robbers' pounding footsteps stopped.

Otto glanced over his shoulder to see officials ushering the Unstoppables on stage. The crowd thought they were real Highland Dancers!

"Dancing robbers?" gasped Otto. This wasn't the plan! The plan was for the Unstoppables to snatch the fake scrapbook. But how *could* they if they were dancing? Otto knew he had to play for time. What could he do? Pretend to drop something? Or, even better, fake a twisted ankle!

Stinkerton looked out from the stage. How were they going to catch those kids if they were doing Highland dancing! Then suddenly he spotted them. But hang on a minute – the boy was on the ground! He was holding his ankle and screwing up his face, as if he was in pain. His sisters were fussing over him, trying to tug him to his feet.

A twisted ankle, thought Stinkerton with a smirk. *What luck!*

Now he knew he could still get the kids. But only if they got this stupid dance out of the way nice and quick.

"Faster!" roared Stinkerton to the bagpiping musicians. "Play faster!"

The music speeded up and the robbers hurtled through their dance. People in the crowd were frowning and muttering, as they hopped over swords like they were dancing on hot coals. The Unstoppables twirled at breakneck speed, cupping their hands above their heads like ballerinas!

"When is this stupid dance going to finish!" Stinkerton hissed to his sidekicks.

"Not soon enough for me!" Lenny glowered.

"Whoohoo!" beamed Doug, spinning so fast that his skirt fanned out around him.

"Arrgh!" gasped the audience, covering their eyes as Doug flashed a pair of dotty red pants.

"Pack it in! You're overdoing it!" hissed Lenny.

"Wheee!" cried Doug, spinning even faster.

Finally the jaunty music stopped. The robbers bowed, then leaped off the stage. They bounded towards the children, who were still fussing over the boy's ankle.

"Ha!" roared Stinkerton, swiping Otto's rucksack and making off with it through the crowd. "To our hideout!" he called to his sidekicks. Lenny raced right after him but Doug was still skipping.

"Leave off with that stupid dancing, Doug!" yelled Lenny.

The moment the robbers were out of sight, Otto sprang to his feet. "Brilliant!" he beamed. "They've got the rucksack *and* the fake scrapbook inside it!"

"All thanks to you," Martha nodded. "It was

genius, the way you faked that twisted ankle. They didn't guess that we were stalling *one* bit!"

"So far, so good!" Scarlett grinned.

The plan was going like clockwork.

Chapter ELEVEN

"Dang and blast!" exploded Stinkerton. "I do not *believe* it! Those infernal kids have tricked us yet again!"

The Unstoppables were in their tent, staring gloomily at the fake scrapbook.

"Those little monsters!" Stinkerton snarled. "I'll get those kids if it's the last thing I do!"

Furiously, he flung the book away. But as it hit the mouldy tent wall, a folded-up bit of paper fell out and floated to the ground.

"What's that?" grunted Doug, picking it up.

"Give it to me!" bellowed Stinkerton.

"All right! All right!" puffed Doug. "Keep your sporran on!"

Stinkerton snatched it. "It's a note!" he said, reading what Otto had written. "What a nerve," he boomed. "Those kids are trying to ... *blackmail* us!"

He would have done exactly the same if he had been in their shoes. But how dare someone try to con *him*. Those kids were pulling his strings like he was their puppet!

Stinkerton scratched his sweaty moustache. How could it *ever* have got to this? Stuck in a tent and being ordered about by a bunch of kooky kids! "Arrghhhh!" he roared, hitting his forehead. "I *hate* them!" He balled his fists. "I have *got* to get my book back! Or we'll all go to jail, do you hear me!"

"What's the plan then, gov?" asked Doug.

"Plan?" hissed Stinkerton, looking fit to burst. "We don't need a *plan*, you great doughnut! We just go to that barn and get the *real* book back."

Doug scratched his head. "No plan?"

"But— But—" spluttered Lenny. "We *always* have a plan. How will we know what to do?"

"QUIET!" roared Stinkerton. "You just do what I tell you, like always!"

The children spent the afternoon watching Highland Games events with Aunt Beastly and Basil. Then, around teatime, Aunt Beastly took them off to the food tent.

As they were waiting to be served, a curly-haired man marched up and barged in front.

"Excuse me!" Aunt Beastly boomed. "There *is* a queue, you know."

"But I need to eat," the man boomed back in a strong Welsh accent. "I don't want to boast, but I'm Ifor Ramm, a champion caber-tosser and when I need food, that's that!"

Aunt Beastly bristled. "Well, we all need to eat. Basil here is positively *starving!*"

"But he's just a pig," sniffed Ifor Ramm. He rippled his mountainous muscles. "Here, look at *these*," Ifor nodded. "Muscles like these don't grow on trees. I need proper food to keep them *stunning*!"

"Pah!" snapped Aunt Beastly. "I've got muscles, too, though I don't feel the need to go rippling them! And Basil, I will have you know, is not a *pig* in the slightest, but a very rare tufty-tailed boar!"

"He's a pig!" Ifor roared, grabbing a pasty while Mary was still out in the kitchen. He slammed some coins down on the counter and raised his eyebrows at Basil. "And my armpits are tuftier than his scrawny tail!" Then he turned and marched away.

"How ... how *dare* you!" spat Aunt Beastly.

Mary bustled back out of the kitchen and Aunt Beastly ordered scrambled eggs for Basil and four portions of the Games Special for the rest of them.

As Mary handed over their meals, the children wrinkled up their noses.

"What *is* it?" asked Scarlett, peering at her plate.

"Haggis, neeps and tatties," snapped Mary. "It's a Scottish delicacy. And mind you eat up every bit!"

"I'll see that they do!" called Aunt Beastly, striding off to a table.

"No!" wailed the children. "We're not ea—"

"Because if you don't," continued Aunt Beastly, "Mary will be most displeased! And trust me, you wouldn't want to make *her* cross."

The children glanced at Mary, who was watching them through eagle-sharp eyes. They picked up their forks and prodded their haggis, which was the colour of mud.

"Well, don't blame me if I'm sick," said Scarlett. She frowned at Basil, as the nasty little beast started wolfing down his yummy scrambled egg. "Can't we just have some of that?"

"Eat up!" Aunt Beastly snapped.

After a positively tortuous tea, they plodded back outside. Otto climbed on to a stack of hay bales to have a good look around. It was getting dark but it wasn't quite sunset yet.

He saw the TV crews down at the loch setting up their cameras. Otto hoped that Rattlebones would make Loch Greythorn as famous as Loch Ness. Then all the villagers would be happy, like before.

Suddenly Aunt Beastly was calling again. The caber-tossing final was taking place and she was keen to go and watch. They hurried over to see the muscly men and women flinging massive tree trunks through the air.

"What do they actually have to do?" asked Martha. It looked so very dangerous!

"They must turn their caber in the air," said Aunt Beastly, "and get it to land pointing straight up. Like a clock hand in the twelve o'clock position."

A big man with dark, curly hair then stepped

up and threw his tree trunk with ease. He waited until it landed *almost* dead straight. Then he strutted round rippling his muscles.

"Hang on – it's *him*!" Aunt Beastly boomed. "That ghastly man from the food tent!"

She watched the head judge measure the caber's position and nod to all the other judges.

"I don't believe it," Aunt Beastly barked. "That idiot's going to win! Huh!" she snorted. "Over my dead body!"

Ifor was just seconds away from being crowned champion when Aunt Beastly plonked Basil into Otto's arms and yelled, "Wait!"

The children froze, as people all around turned and stared at them. Otto felt his cheeks turn post-box red.

"I can do better than him!" barked Aunt Beastly, pointing a fat finger at Ifor.

"Yeah, right!" someone shouted.

The muttering crowd weighed up Aunt Beastly, slowly shaking their heads.

"It's true!" snapped Aunt Beastly. She looked at Ifor. "And I'll show you, too – if you're not too *scared* to let me try..."

"Ha ha!" tittered Ifor. "I'm quivering in my boots!" He rippled his muscles. "Be my guest!"

With that, the head judge hurried over. "You can throw straighter than *Ifor Ramm*?"

"Easy peasy!" said Aunt Beastly, with a sniff.

The judge blinked. "Well, madam," he said. "This is most unusual. But if Ifor is willing for you to try..."

Angus and Donald, and Mora and Barry were all in the crowd behind. "Woohoo!" they cheered, waving their flags. "Go, Bessie!"

Aunt Beastly rolled up her thick woollen

sleeves and marched into the arena. She looked like a fearsome gladiator preparing to wrestle an angry lion. Her eyes were narrowed and her nostril hair twitched. She scooped up the hefty tree trunk as if it were a mere twig! Then off she pounded towards the throw line.

Aunt Beastly let her caber fly with an ear-splitting...

"RAGGGGHHHHHHHHH!"

As the tree trunk soared through the air, the confident smile fell from Ifor's face. It landed *dead straight* and the crowd went mad, waving their flags and cheering.

"The lady wins!" cried the judge.

"Hurrah!" the crowd whooped wildly.

Aunt Beastly collected her large rosette and turned round to Ifor. "Better luck next year!" she said with a grin. "Try eating more cabbage and fewer pasties. Goodbye!"

She marched away with Basil and the children down to the loch, where the tug-of-war was taking place.

Two enemy clans were fighting it out – the *Dunroaming Drifters* and the *Torrhooly Tigers*.

As the children watched, they were feeling very twitchy. It was nearly sunset. Very soon they would have to face the Unstoppables.

"What if the robbers don't show up?" whispered Scarlett.

"They will," said Otto firmly.

"Here," murmured Martha. And she gave them each a small, black lucky-fluffle cat. "To keep you safe when we face the robbers," she whispered.

But first they had to get away from Aunt Beastly. They waited until she was showing off her rosette to one of the tug-of-war judges, then Otto hurried up to her and said very quickly... "We need the loo – be back soon!" And he made to run away.

"Hold on a moment!" Aunt Beastly trilled. "I need the toilet, too."

But at that moment, another judge appeared, asking to see Aunt Beastly's rosette.

"Of course!" she smiled, rippling her muscles. She glanced at Otto and called across. "All right, dear – off you go! But don't be long or you'll miss the rowing race."

"Okay!" Otto and his sisters hurried off.

The navy blue sky was now streaked with peach as the sun dropped over the hills. They raced down the bank and stopped at the barn door to check that no one was watching.

"Coast's clear!" panted Otto, and they quickly slipped inside.

The darkness of the barn engulfed them. Martha got the torches out of her rucksack and they turned them on.

But Otto knew the robbers could arrive at any second. "Come on," he said to his sisters. "Into position."

They had talked about where they all needed to be, so nobody asked any questions. On his way, Otto took the real scrapbook from its hiding place and stuffed it up his jumper.

He was certain that the Unstoppables would want to see it, to make sure they weren't being tricked. That was always how it worked in *Montague Plum's Mysteries*.

Scarlett made sure her Creeper-Sneakers were done up nice and tight. She switched them on and, clutching Fred, she climbed up one of the walls and walked, upside down, along the highest rafter.

When she was exactly over the spot where Otto would lure the Unstoppables, Scarlett stopped and hung from the rafter like a bat. As long as she remembered to keep very quiet, no one would ever spot her.

Martha looked suddenly worried as her sister dangled there. "I hope they get here soon," she said, "or Scarlett's brain will drip out of her ears!"

"No, it won't," Scarlett giggled. "I hang around from the trees at home for hours!"

Scarlett turned off her torch. Then Martha stepped back across to the door and sent Squawk out into the night sky to watch for the robbers' approach.

"I do hope they come soon," she said. "Or it'll be too dark for Squawk to spot them. Otto, is your screen switched on?"

"Yep," said Otto. He scanned the screen as Squawk soared around outside.

Martha was right. As the sky grew darker, it was getting quite tricky to make people out.

"Okay," whispered Otto. "Now all we have to do is wait..."

Chapter TWELVE

The children waited five minutes. They waited ten. After fifteen minutes the robbers still hadn't shown up. Otto kept checking the screen on his tracker watch but couldn't see them anywhere.

"Where *are* they?" muttered Scarlett impatiently.

The children could now hear fireworks outside. Day one of the Games was nearly over.

"They're not coming, are they?" Martha murmured.

Then Otto spotted something on the screen and zoomed in. Three dark figures. "Shhh," he whispered. "It's them! Robbers located and heading down the bank. They're here!"

Martha ran into position just behind Otto but with a clear escape route to the door. As soon as the robbers were captured in Scarlett's net, she'd need to race out and get help.

There was silence. Then...

C-r-e-a-k. The barn door edged open and three figures stepped inside.

A blinding light burned Otto's eyes as the Unstoppables shone their powerful torch beams right into his face.

He could just make them out, edging towards him through the murky gloom. Otto felt his heart begin to thump and his hands go cold and clammy.

The robbers stopped.

"Two kids?" said Stinkerton, looking from Otto to Martha. "Where's the other one – the freckly red-headed little horror?"

"Um, not here," Otto replied.

"Why not?"

"She's f-feeling sick!" Martha chipped in, with every bit of nerve she had.

Up on her rafter high above, Scarlett dangled down. In her hand was Fred and her finger was poised above his *supersonic net-shoot* button.

A little horror? Right! thought Scarlett. *I'll show them!*

"The scrapbook," said Stinkerton, his eyes fixed on Otto. His voice was cool but Otto detected a slight tremor.

"The money first," Otto answered. He tried to sound like Plum and it seemed to work. Stinkerton slipped his hand into his pocket and pulled out a wad of money.

Breathing hard, Otto held out his hand but Stinkerton jerked the notes away.

"Not until I see the scrapbook!" he snapped.

"Too right," growled Lenny and Doug.

Otto was determined to hold his nerve. He didn't really want their money – that was just to

206

make the whole thing look real.

Okay, he thought. He would show them the book but *not* let them hold it. He hoped that Scarlett was concentrating though. When Otto coughed, that was the signal for Scarlett to shoot down the net. Then the robbers would be caught like flies in a spider's web.

Otto slid out the scrapbook from under his jumper.

"Give it to me!" Stinkerton commanded. "The book – hand it over. NOW!"

Otto held on tight but to his horror Stinkerton started walking around him. Otto heard the robber's footsteps stop behind him and he spun round to face him. But now Stinkerton was in the wrong position for when Scarlett shot down the net. All three robbers had to be together – back *in front of him* – for this to work.

As Otto considered what he should do, Stinkerton made a dive for the scrapbook.

"Hey!" yelled Otto, jumping back.

But Lenny and Doug were waiting behind. They grabbed him and held on tight.

"No!" squeaked Martha, dashing towards them. "Stop!"

Stinkerton swiped the book clean out of Otto's hands.

Otto coughed loudly. Scarlett *had* to send the net down now or the robbers would get away. But everyone was in the wrong place!

Fwip! The net tumbled down, straight on to ... *Martha and Otto!*

"Argghhh!" they shrieked, trying to fight their way out and getting more and more tangled.

"Ha!" laughed Stinkerton. "You thought you'd catch us?" He flicked his torch to the rafters, as an upside-down Scarlett hurried back along the beam. "You and your tinpot inventions!" he roared. "Pathetic!"

With the scrapbook clutched tightly in his hands, Stinkerton fled to the door. Lenny and Doug were hot on his heels. They had won!

Outside, the firework extravaganza was being broadcast to the nation, but Stinkerton had no eyes for the show. All he cared about *now* was the book in his hands. His beautiful, beloved scrapbook! Relief flooded through him like a great tidal wave, filling him with happiness.

He forgot about the Crumbs. He forgot about the crowds. He forgot about the TV cameras.

"I'm brilliant!" Stinkerton called to the stars, waving his book in the air. "Sebastian Stinkerton! The greatest robber in the world!"

"Gov," whispered Lenny.

"I'm a star! I'm a criminal mastermind! There's no one as cunning as me!"

"Stop!" hissed Doug, prodding his arm.

"No one will EVER stop us!" beamed Stinkerton. "Because we are the Un—"

"STOP!" Doug clamped his podgy hand over Stinkerton's mouth.

Stinkerton reeled. And then the leader of the Unstoppables started to come to his senses...

"Oh no," he gasped, blinking, as he suddenly noticed the crowd. They were watching.

Watching *him*. And a TV camera was pointing straight at him...

"What did I say? What did I *say*?" Stinkerton banged his forehead.

The crowd was now pointing and muttering.

"I didn't mean..." Stinkerton gulped. "It was just ... just a joke." He swallowed hard. As far as he could remember, he hadn't actually *said* that they were...

"The Unstoppables!" came a cry.

It was Martha. She was racing out of the barn with her brother and sister at her side.

"The Unstoppables!" she yelled again.

Aunt Beastly barged to the front of the crowd with Basil stuffed under her arm. "The UNSTOPPABLES?" she boomed, her voice full of anger. "How dare they show their faces again! After everything that happened in the museum!"

"Well, they did!" shouted Scarlett. "And they *even* called me a little horror! What a cheek!"

As fireworks popped and banged in the sky, Aunt Beastly advanced on the robbers.

"Run!" squeaked Stinkerton. But where could they go? The crowd was blocking their route across the fields and the only thing behind them was the loch.

Then he spied a single rowing boat on the water's edge. "HA!" he panted, sprinting towards it.

Lenny and Doug followed. They dived in and Doug started to row.

"Faster!" yelled Stinkerton, clutching his scrapbook. "Faster!"

The crowd rushed to the edge of the water but all the other boats were on the far side of the loch, where they'd been left after the boat race.

"*What now?*" said Scarlett.

The robbers were escaping. It was all over.

"There must be *something* we can do!" Otto cried. And then, quite suddenly, he spotted Hamish. "Wait a minute," he gasped, swallowing hard. "*Rattlebones!*"

The crowd watched the robbers' boat speed across the water. As the twinkling sparkles of exploding fireworks lit the dark sky, a cluster of giant bubbles appeared on the surface of the loch.

Then, a great groaning sound from deep underwater made everyone gasp.

"What's that noise?" a man shouted.

"Something's under the water!" a woman yelled.

"What is it?" shrieked a little boy.

It sounded like an angry giant had woken in a towering temper.

And then she rose, red-eyed and fearsome. Rattlebones burst up out of the loch, her silhouette filling the smoky sky.

"*Look! A monster!*" the crowd cried.

But no sooner had they glimpsed the beast than she slipped under the water and was gone.

The monster's body had whipped up the water and sent the little boat holding the Unstoppables spinning round and round. As they were trying to steady her, waves rippled across the loch.

"Arggh!" they cried.

A huge wave toppled the boat over with a giant *SPLASH!* and the Unstoppables disappeared under the water.

Seconds passed. The boat was floating upside down but there was no sign of the robbers.

"They've drowned," Martha murmured.

"No, they haven't!" Scarlett cried. "Look – *there!*"

The robbers' heads had broken the surface of the water.

"Help! Save us!" spluttered Lenny and Doug.

"My scrapbook!" yelled Stinkerton. "Where ... where *is* it?"

As his sidekicks thrashed about, Stinkerton looked around frantically. "My precious scrapbook!" he roared again. "*IT'S GONE!*"

Chapter
THIRTEEN

B y the next morning, the Crumb children were
heroes. Because of them the Unstoppables
were safely behind bars. It really didn't matter
that Stinkerton's scrapbook was rotting beneath
the murky water, as there was video evidence of
his accidental confession.

After an awful lot of explaining, Aunt Beastly
had forgiven the children for not involving her in
their plan. So now their aunt knew everything.

Well, *almost* everything. The children hadn't
mentioned that Rattlebones wasn't real, for that
was not *their* secret to give away. And so Aunt
Beastly, like the rest of the world, believed that
Loch Greythorn had a monster – one that had
helped protect Muldoon from the Unstoppables.

Martha, Otto and Scarlett had been invited
to do a live TV interview. The whole nation,
it seemed, was itching to find out how three

young kids had managed to bring down the most notorious baddies in history...

"Easy!" said Scarlett to the TV reporter, when the cameras had just started rolling. "The cowardly robbers dived into the loch simply to get away from *me*. But anyway, I'm friends with the monster who lives there and she's no—"

"Scarlett!" Otto cried, before his sister blurted out the secret. "Er, what Scarlett really means is that she'd *like* to be friends with the monster – i-if sea monsters *had* friends."

Otto glared at Scarlett, who poked out her tongue but stayed silent.

"I don't like monsters," said Martha vaguely. "Especially ones that live down plugholes. Those ones are the *very* worst kind." She looked at the reporter with big, round eyes.

He cleared his throat. "So, anyway..." he said,

as his right eye started to twitch, "you came to Scotland to stay with your aunt?"

"Yep – and the boars!" said Scarlett, with a groan. "There are forty of them now but none have tufty tails. Not a single one!"

"But the robbers! The robbers!" yelled the reporter. "Tell me about *the robbers*!"

"*They* don't have tufty tails *either*," scowled Scarlett. "That's just silly!"

The reporter shook his head and frowned. "Well, the nation's *so* grateful to you for putting those criminals in jail."

"That's okay," said Otto. "Though Squawk helped, too – he's my spy-bird."

"Nice interview, children!" Aunt Beastly beamed, once the camera had stopped rolling. "You came across as beautifully normal!"

They wandered over to the Games field to catch some of the events taking place on day two. There was an exciting stone-hurling event, followed by a bit of "normal" Highland dancing, without a robber in sight. Finally, they went to the food tent to get a drink.

"Oh!" said Mary, as they stood at the counter. "Isn't it a glorious day!"

"Yes," smiled Aunt Beastly. "My, *you* look happy!"

"And so I should be!" Mary grinned. "So should we *all*, you know! Haven't you heard? Since the monster-sighting, the phones in Muldoon haven't stopped ringing. Tourists are flocking in from far and wide. All the rooms in Angus's pub are booked up for months ahead. And Mora and Barry's wee guest house, too. Then there's Hamish – he's going to start monster-spotting tours on the loch!"

"Wonderful!" Aunt Beastly boomed. "And everyone must come and see my amazing tufty-tailed boars! When their little tails tuft, that is..."

"Aye," sniffed Mary. "And as for me – well, as soon as the Games finish tomorrow I'll be opening my tea room again. I cannee wait for that!" She looked at the children. "Who's for some free cream buns, then?"

"Really?" said Aunt Beastly. "Well, how kind!"

"Not *you*," said Mary. "Just them kiddies." Then she broke into a wheezy laugh. "Only joking!"

As they ate the most delicious cream tea, Otto slipped out his notebook. Keeping it carefully hidden under the table, he flicked to a nice clean page near the back and scribbled down:

Case 433

But what would his next case be...?